IMMORTAL FULFILLMENT

AN IMMORTAL STORY OF TRUE
LOVE, DISCOVERY, AND LIFE

The Immortal Stories Series

Book 2

by

Linda Ashton Trott

Tagger Press

Copyright

ISBN-13: 978-1-7781131-3-0

Cover design by: 100COVERS

Version 2, December 2022

Adult Content, 18+

Dedication

I am dedicating this book to my husband, who without, it would have been impossible to complete this work.

A huge thank you to Lee Burton for being my editor. On my second book, I am still learning and he is a very good teacher and editor.

Another thank you goes out to Dawn Hughes for being my continuity editor. On a series, this is a tantamount and difficult task!

Thanks to you the reader as well, for purchasing this book. I hope you enjoy it! If you do, don't forget to leave a review.

Contents

Author's Note

In light of the changes to Book 1 - Immortal Desire, we took a look at book 2, and changed the beginning a bit to make it better than before.

What did you miss?

In the previous Immortal Story

- Falon met Zisis, an Immortal being.

- Zisis helped Falon escape from a bad marriage.

- Zisis's family forces him to leave Falon behind.

- Falon picks her life up, and gets a new job and apartment.

- Falon has first adventure, working in New York.

- She lives through some scary situations while traveling.

- Falon meets Mark, a business man from Texas.

- Mark comes to Montreal for a visit – steamy times!

- Falon gets second adventure working in Atlanta, GA.

- Mark reveals a secret, and breaks Falon's heart.

1—Hurricanes

I woke up before the alarm this morning with the breath of yet another dream of Mark and I having sex that turned me into a vampire. Shaking, I got out of bed and went to the window. The sky looked strange, not a color I had ever seen before. It was the beginning of the summer in Georgia.

Why was I having dreams like that? Because of what Mark had explained to me, that's why. He's not freaking human! Mark or Zisis or whatever he wants to call himself is a freaking alien from another planet! I can't think about this now. What's happening with the sky?

When the radio came on it was a warning that a hurricane was heading toward the Georgia coastline. Now this was not unusual for July in Georgia. Still, it was a little scary for me as I had never been close to a hurricane before. The radio's weather report said it was not likely to hit as far inland as Atlanta, but all flights had been canceled or delayed departing for Florida and coastline cities.

Actually, it was more than a little scary. It was enough to divert my thoughts.

I turned on the television to see if there were any local weather broadcasts. Flipping through the channels, I discovered one that was local, and they had someone on the coast in Savannah. The cameraman was pointing out to sea. The picture showed a huge black mass of clouds on the horizon and a very angry sea pounding the beach.

The storm was currently a Category 2 but they expected it to get stronger as it tracked northward. The current landfall projections placed it just north of Jacksonville, Florida, with it curving up and along the coast. However, the radar showed that as far inland as Atlanta could be inundated with heavy rain. People were told to stay indoors and to avoid travel. Coastal communities were being evacuated now because the storm was due to hit within the hour.

It sure looked close! I left the television on while I went to get my shower. I figured I would keep an eye on what was happening, then call up to the office before I left for breakfast. If they advised me not to come into work, then I would work here today.

The water sluiced over my head, nice and hot. I closed my eyes and just let the water course over my head and shoulders. Pretty soon, I forgot about the storm raging out at sea and just relaxed.

Unfortunately, as happened often these past weeks, my mind started to go back over what happened between me and Mark in May. I replayed the scene in my head again.

"Zisis? What the fuck!"

"Yes, I am Zisis, and Mark," he said, changing back into Mark in front of me.

"Speak plainly! I don't understand. What is going on?"

"I have an explanation for you, but it is crazy, and you have to understand that it is a secret. You can't tell anyone, ever. I'm only telling you because I love you and you deserve an explanation. But the explanation will likely drive you crazy."

"That sounds crazy, you know?"

"Yup. "So here goes: I'm not of this world," he started. *"I'm not human. I am a member of a species that came to Earth before the end of the last ice age. We are for all intents and purposes, immortal. We live very long lives. Some of the myths about vampires and werewolves were based on us. We aren't supernatural per se, just a different species—a hominid that developed differently than homo sapiens. We have fangs, but they are not for drinking blood. They are more like weapons when fighting or for subduing a female during coitus."*

"The unusual things you noticed were real. I do have inhuman strength. We can change the way we look. We are stronger than humans and heal faster. We also see better, hear better, scent better. In fact, all of our senses are sharper, plus we have a couple of extra senses. Some of us have special talents like mind-reading or telekinesis. We have always lived among humans but we hide because ... well, in the past, humans were afraid of us and hunted us."

"And the biting and the fangs?" I asked. *"What the fuck are they?"* Like I believe any of this!

"The fangs are vestigial, a throwback to an earlier evolution, a time when we were more wild and sex was more animalistic. Just like big cats, we bite down on our females to prevent escape and to provide aid in the form of a chemical that is pleasure-inducing. In short, it helps the female experience a cosmic orgasm."

Well, that's true. I can attest to that bit of information. Cosmic indeed.

"The venom has two purposes; it's used to turn humans and it helps our youth complete their transition and it's used as a defensive weapon to kill our enemies."

"What do you mean, turn humans?"

"When we bite a human and give them enough venom, it starts the process of transmogrification—or transforming them into one of us," he explained.

"Is that what happened when you bit me?" I asked. "Am I turning into one of you?"

"No, I don't think so. I have to give you a lot for the transformation to be triggered."

"How much is a lot?" I asked.

"Everything I have until I'm empty."

I relived those moments of the last time we made love; the intensity, the highs. I had taken control and pushed him until he became an animal. He took me so roughly that my body responded in a way I hadn't realized it could. It was immensely satisfying, and I couldn't get enough. Until he bit me. I remember the sensation of his fangs sinking into my shoulder, the momentary pain being inundated with the wave of pleasure that followed. I now know it was the venom. I had floated on that wave, while my body had orgasm after orgasm, until I was weak and spent. I was a bag of mush—albeit happy mush.

Just remembering them, I touched myself and found my body wanting him. I was sensitive and wet, eager for his touch.

He had called me his mated true love. I certainly felt like he was my true love, but can I trust a man that lied to me so completely? What am I saying, he's not even a man! But oh God, I loved him, my body loved him, I needed him like air. How sad is that?

"What happens now?" I had asked. I was watching his face, hearing, but not yet absorbing the consequences.

"I don't know," he answered. "I have never been here before."

"Am ... am I going to die?" I asked. I had just realized this could kill me. He might have killed me with that bite. "How long do I have?"

My fear then turned into anger. It was beginning to flow through me, a slow boil that started to burn all the feelings away. He should have told me before he bit me! I should have had a choice!

"I think you should go now," I said very quietly.

Mark got dressed and left the room without another word.

I had been so furious, and now I was shaking all over again. The last thing I had asked him was if I would die. I hadn't yet, so I guess not. I needed space, time, and quiet to process this mess. I told him to leave. At least he did that, without argument.

I had sat there attempting to pull myself away from an edge I hadn't expected to be at.

Why? Why is this happening again? What the fuck?

I sat there asking questions that didn't have answers.

All I had known was that I wasn't going there. He wasn't going to break me again.

All Mark had told me, had shown me, was swirling around in my head, and I was trying to make sense of it. Mark had crossed a boundary that I wasn't even aware was there.

What was nastier was that he was now my boss, for God's sake. *How creepy is that? Geez!*

But that wasn't the worst. He was Zisis! Or was Zisis Mark?

My eyes snapped open. It was another reverie, reliving that moment when, yet again, my world was pulled out from under me like a rug.

No! Not going there again. You are stronger this time. You are a new person. You are not the victim you were. Hold your head high!

I finished up my shower and got dressed. The TV said the storm was still on the same track as before. So it was time to go eat and get my day organized.

I headed down to the dining room. The place was pretty full, but there was a table left in the back. Everyone was talking about the impending hurricane. Both tourists and businesspeople were concerned with traveling with this storm coming in.

Downstairs, Franco waved good morning to me. Janelle was playing hostess for breakfast today. She led me to the last table and asked me if I wanted the usual. Nodding, I asked her if there was an update on the hurricane.

"Yeah, they think it may dump three inches of rain on us today. There will be flooding all over the place."

"Ouch, that's not good!" I said. "Is the hotel at risk?"

"No, not really. We're on pretty high ground here. You'd best stay here today, 'cause there's gonna be a messa trouble outside!"

I thanked her for the advice and read my book until my food arrived. Listening to the murmuring voices at the other tables, I had to concur with Janelle's advice, so I decided to see what my boss Ray would prefer when I got back to my room. Ray was the project manager for this Atlanta project. He wasn't my direct boss, that was still Peter in Montreal, but I reported to Ray while down here. He was on the customer side of things.

When I returned to my room, there was a flashing light on the phone, indicating a message. It was from Ray, so I called the office.

"Hello, Ray, you rang?" I asked when he answered.

"Ya, hon, you'd best not drive into the office today as there's to be a big blow here. They're now saying it could be a Cat 4 by tomorrow. Wouldn't want ya to get drowned now, would we?"

"Okay, I'll work here then today. I brought a laptop with me so that I can learn that piece of software you gave me yesterday. Perhaps I can work on that and get the project cycle documented."

"That would be ideal, Falon," he said. "We'll see you tomorrow, then, or after the storm passes, whichever comes first."

Hanging up the phone, I went to the television and turned off the volume so that I could focus. Opening up my laptop, I brought the reports to the table to start work. However, an hour into the work, my mind was wandering again.

Mark was Zisis.

Zisis was Mark! How could he lie to me like that? How could he not tell me? How could he?

What do I call him now?

I mean, I had to admit that something was bothering me. There were more than a couple of times I'd found myself comparing Mark to Zisis. I thought it was my imagination, that it was wishful thinking. Or worse, that I was losing my mind. But they seemed so close.

But I wasn't. It was all real. He was him. Even though he looked different, it was still him.

When Mark had finished his explanation and told me what he "had to", I was so angry that I had grown very quiet. I was like my mom that way, the angrier I got the quieter I got. I was too angry to say anything, and I hadn't wanted to say anything I would regret, so I had clamped my mouth shut and quietly asked him to leave.

That was the end of May. It was now July. I needed to get past this. I needed to decide if I could forgive him. *Do I want to forgive him? I'm still so angry.*

Except, there was no denying that I had fallen for him, and he still loved me. Was that enough? The sex was perfect. But was perfect sex a reason to have a relationship with someone?

No.

There has to be trust. Trust. He lied to me. He lied to me for five months. *No, he lied to me for nearly five years!* All that time I spent broken, crying myself to sleep.

AARHG! No, don't go there again. Break this cycle of thought.

Pulling myself out of my reverie again, I looked back at my report. I needed to get the first draft done before lunch. *So get to it!*

I closed my laptop after sending the draft report to Ray. I glanced at the clock and saw it was lunchtime. I stood, stretched, and went to the window to look out.

All I could see was rain, great sheets of it driving down to the ground at such a strange angle at first I thought the building was tilting. The wind was blowing the drops across the glass sideways instead of to the ground. The world seemed upside down.

From the vantage point of the tenth floor, the horizon was usually clear and a long way off. Today, there was nothing. I couldn't even see the parking lot below or the buildings in the distance. It was just sheets of rain. Even the buildings across the street were obscured and blurred.

A strong curiosity overcame me at that moment. I wanted to go up to the pool deck. I wanted to experience the fury of my first-ever hurricane firsthand. So I grabbed my room key and took the elevator up the two levels to the rooftop pool. When I exited the elevator, I could hear the howling of the wind even more. For a second I almost changed my mind—but I kept going forward.

I opened the door of the belvedere and peeked outside. The doorway was on the lee side of the building, so the wind wasn't blowing directly into the door. However, the rain was still extremely heavy here. I was instantly soaked to the skin. The rain was cold too, not like the normal rain you get in July in the South.

Since trying to stay dry was now pointless, I decided to go outside completely. Checking to make sure the door was not locked, I left the safety of the belvedere and stepped out onto the pool deck. There was no one there, of course. The pool was deserted, and all the chairs, tables, and umbrellas were safely put away.

Stepping around the corner of the belvedere, I was blasted by hurricane-force winds. They almost blew me off my feet. I had to hang on to the building to gain my balance.

Exhilarated by the danger, I let go of the building and started to walk across the deck. There was a large gazebo by the pool that was solid looking, so I made for it. I was completely bent over at the waist trying to make myself smaller so I wasn't as much of a sail to the wind. I hugged the big posts that were anchored in the concrete for all I was worth and let the storm rage around me. It blew my hair into wet tails, and pushed my face around. The raindrops felt like BB gun pellets hitting my face and body. It stung like crazy.

Even hanging onto the post, the wind was so strong it pushed me off my feet. The rain was now leaving marks on my skin. It felt like hail and there were tiny balls of ice collecting on the roof.

I stood there under the gazebo staring at the pool. The water level had reached the edge and was starting to spill over. I felt the building gently swaying in the wind too. That in itself wasn't scary; tall buildings were designed to do that. But the movement of the building was making the water slosh from side to side like tea in a teacup you're carrying.

Thoughts jumped into my head:

What happens to the water in a pool when it overflows? What happens if the water sloshes over the side? Will the pool deck collapse?

A number of disaster movies ran through my head. I easily saw the entire volume of water jumping out of the pool and rushing down the building. Or better yet, the pool crashing through the roof down to the floors below. Yikes, my room was underneath!

All I could think of was tens of thousands of gallons of water crashing through the ceiling of my room as the pool fell through the roof.

I looked around for a phone. I figured there had to be a house phone up here somewhere—even if it was just for the staff. There! At the bar!

I made my way to the bar and hunched down behind the counter after I grabbed the phone. I dialed the front desk.

"Front desk," said the clerk.

"I'm up here on the roof by the pool," I screamed into the phone over the noise of the storm. "The pool! It looks like it's about to overflow! Someone has to do something!"

Static came back through the phone because I couldn't hear anything.

"Come quick!" I yelled, and then hung up.

Ten minutes later, two people fought their way across the pool deck toward me. They were having as much trouble as I did. When they reached me, it was a maintenance man and someone else.

The maintenance man went immediately to the pool maintenance shed and started to work on something. I heard a large motor start up and then a huge whoosh as a lot of water cascaded over the edge of the building.

The other man came over to me, he appeared to be one of the concierges.

"Hi there," he yelled over the screaming wind. "Are you okay?"

"I'm fine. What is he doing?" I pointed at the water.

"There is a storm release that should have been triggered to let excess water out of the pool in the event of a bad storm. So we're glad you noticed!" he yelled. "Let me get you back to safety."

He took me by the elbow and led me back to the belvedere. Once we were inside, he handed over a few large towels that he had left there at the ready.

"What were you thinking going out there today?" he asked me.

"Yeah, it was pretty stupid. In my defense, I've never seen a hurricane and I wanted to experience the storm personally." I shrugged. "I needed to clear my head and didn't think it would be so dangerous."

"Well, now you know," he smiled. "You could have been blown off the roof."

"Do you really think so?" Then I remembered just how easily the wind had tossed me about. I realized I was probably very lucky. "Well, it didn't happen. All's well," I said glibly.

"Please don't do that again!" he said earnestly.

"I won't."

"I recommend a hot bath to warm up, and then come on down to the hotel bar for some great music."

"Sounds like a plan."

2—Sober Second Thought

Back in my room I had a long hot bath. What a luxury to have enough hot water to fill a soaker tub! As I lay there in the water I could see tiny ripples in the surface from the concussion of the wind on the building. The water was sloshing ever so slightly from side to side. I had filled the tub almost to the top. Now, I thought I'd better drain some out. I felt spoiled by the hotel; my hot water tank at home never could give me this much hot water. It would go cold about half filled, leaving me without.

Sitting there soaking, I started shaking from the shock of the reality that I could have died up there on that roof. What was I thinking? *Stupid, stupid, stupid!*

Was I being stupid about Mark too? Was this easier than I thought? *Am I making too much of something I shouldn't be?*

Stepping out of the tub, I stood in front of the full-length mirror in the bathroom assessing myself.

I've got nicely shaped breasts. They're big, but not huge. Guys like the fullness of them and I like how responsive they are. My waist is slim, but I have flesh on my hips and legs. I've got a big full ass. My legs are strong as a result of being a competitive skater.

I'm not tall, but that's an advantage for a woman. I love my auburn hair, and my face isn't bad. I've never been a beauty, but I have nice eyes. They are a deep blue now, but they can lighten to almost a sky blue. All in all, I thought I'm a pretty good catch.

Wrapping myself in the fluffy bathrobe, I wrapped a towel around my hair and walked over to the windows. I stood there staring out at the storm. In May:

I felt numb.

I felt angry.

I felt abandoned again.

I was so hurt, I could barely breathe.

I told Mark to leave, and he did without a word. That was good. The last thing I could have handled was him starting to argue with me. I needed space—clarity.

He told me a story about immortals and rules. He said he did want to hurt me. *Is this what he meant?*

The memories of Zisis had faded but this with Mark, was sharp and pointy. The reality of some of the things that had happened faded too. Somehow my mind had put them under the "your imagination" column and left them there.

Strange things had happened more than once. Had they all been Mark aka Zisis 'watching over me'?

I need to call Lora. She is my best friend, confident, and a witch. Her brand of witchcraft is love magic and her superpower is making connections with people.

"Hi hun, how are you doing? How is Atlanta?" asked Lora.

"Atlanta is nice, hot, steamy weather right now. We're in the middle of a hurricane. I went up on the roof to experience it."

"You did what? Are you nuts?"

"I guess I must be — you're the second person that's said that. I needed to clear my head."

"Oh? What happened?"

"Well without getting into too much, Mark and I have had a fight. It was a couple of months ago actually."

"Like back in May?"

"Yeah, at the end of May. He surprised me here and you know, one thing led to another."

"Okay, awesome sex, but why the fight?"

"He admitted to me that he's been lying to me from the beginning. He is not who he said he was, in fact he showed me he's Zisis."

The other end of the line was silent.

"Lora?"

"Yeah, I'm here, thinking."

"Okay, I'll wait."

"First, do you believe him?"

"I think I can answer yes to that question. The evidence was pretty convincing. His story is the same too."

"Do you believe he loves you?"

"Yes, I believe that too. I can see his love for me."

"Do you love him?"

"I was falling for him. And if I'm really honest with myself, yes, I do."

"Do you trust him?"

"Now, this is where it gets gray. I did trust Mark. In fact, I felt Mark was healing me finally. He never did anything to make me mistrust him. But now? After his confession? I don't know."

"How does he make you feel?"

"He makes me feel loved. We have such a strong connection that I feel like half a person without him. And the sex—oh my God—it was amazing—beyond amazing. It has never been as good with anyone else, except Zisis."

"Well, I think you have your answer then," concluded Lora.

"But is sex enough?" I asked. "Since meeting Mark in New York, we had a lot of sex. It was always mind-blowing, but still really just the beginning of a relationship; in spite of the strongest feelings I have had since Zisis. There is no doubt Mark is my gold standard. Between him and Zisis no other man has measured up—in more than one way."

"It can be. Some women feel lucky just to have awesome sex. Do you want it all? The fairy tale? The Happily Ever After? 'Cause that's what you're debating right now with yourself."

"I am?"

"Yes. If you weren't, you'd be able to move on. It wouldn't matter if he loved you or you loved him. It would just matter if the sex was satisfying. So you're looking for love. If you feel love, you found it. Right?"

"But Mark is Zisis! Ugh!"

"So what?" asked Lora. "What if it had been a witness protection program that took him away. Would you feel so conflicted? Or would you feel grateful you've connected again?"

"Huh! I had not looked at it that way," I answered. "I need to think about this. Thank you, Lora. As always, you help me sort out my crazy thoughts and pour a cold clear bucket of clarity on my head."

"Any time, hun," said Lora. "My personal opinion? I think you just need to have sex with all kinds of men, and forget about forming relationships for now. Have some fun! You're in Atlanta, Georgia – no ties, no commitments, enjoy it."

"I'll consider that too. Bye!"

I got off the phone feeling much more centered and even. It always helps to talk things out with Lora.

So, now my questions are: Do I want love or do I want casual fun? I don't have to worry about honesty and integrity if I'm not looking for a forever guy.

So where does that leave me? Right now, it leaves me with feelings for one man. An immortal whose world is different from mine and has inherent dangers for me. I can set that aside and explore my own self more.

Mark had started to stitch the pieces of my heart back together so that one day I could love again. I'm grateful for that. I really can move on now.

As a sexual partner, Mark fits me in every way—I mean EVERY way.

That's important, ladies, come on! We all know size does count. There's no point in pretending it doesn't. Sure, if there is enough other good stuff about the guy, you can overlook size, but if it's just for pure sex, sorry, size is important. Anyone who says it isn't probably either doesn't have enough experience with other men, or is plain lying!

What started out as rebuilding my life had now become something very different. *Am I ready to love again?* I'd met men down here in the States. I had never expected to find someone I wanted to be with—not for a lifetime. Mark may be that kind of guy, but I owe it to myself to keep looking.

3—Boundaries

A knock on my room door brought me out of my reverie.

"Hello?" I asked through the door. I couldn't see anyone in the peephole.

"Room service."

"I didn't order anything," I said.

"Compliments of the hotel, miss."

I opened the door and a bellhop was there with a tray.

"Hot chocolate and warm fresh biscuits and cream for you."

"Oh my, that sounds lovely," I said. "Please come in." I went to fetch some cash from my purse to give him a tip, but he was gone before I returned.

"This is lovely," I said out loud. I pushed the tray into the sitting room and wheeled it up to the chair and turned on the TV to see what was happening about the storm. Sitting there enjoying my hot chocolate and biscuits, I listened to the newscaster drone on about which areas were inundated with water near the coast. This storm had hit Category 4 before hitting land, but it has again lost power and has been downgraded to a Category 3.

"In other news, an Atlanta hotel narrowly missed a tragic pool accident this afternoon when a guest discovered the pool's automated drain system was not working in the severe wind and rain. A spokesperson for the hotel said that a guest just happened to be in the right place at the right time, sounding the alarm and letting hotel staff solve the problem before it became a tragedy. The automated system, which releases water from the pool in the event of heavy rains, had been shorted out, likely by a lightning strike. If not discovered, the pool would have overrun its walls and flooded the roof, perhaps putting too much weight in one place. The result could have been a collapse."

A video was playing behind the woman showing exactly what she was talking about. It showed an engineering drawing of a rooftop pool collapsing and the water flooding the floors below.

"This could have happened in Atlanta," said the announcer.

"Wow! I made the news," I said aloud. Curling up on the couch, I grabbed my book and read for a while. Eventually my thoughts wandered back to what I was debating with myself.

I needed some boundaries. The problem was that, rightly or wrongly, I had approached these business trips as a license to have fun. I wasn't going to get "serious," because none of these encounters were with someone I would take home with me.

And yet I took Mark home with me.

Maybe I wasn't the type of girl who could distance herself that much. This was supposed to be a fun experience and lighthearted, and non-committal.

Oh, what have I done?

Boundaries. I needed boundaries for myself.

It was very surreal working and living away from home for six months. It was like make-believe. Let's face it, when you're living in a hotel, you're not at your worst. You won't have dirty laundry around, or unwashed dishes. Your cat litter boxes are not there to remind you to clean them. Everything is always nice and tidy. The bed is always made. My bed isn't—at least at home it's not. Some days I simply throw the comforter up and run…

They say the best way to overcome a heartbreak is to get back out there. Clearly, I needed to get Mark out of my system, and that meant meeting more guys.

The clock on the wall said it was 5:00 p.m., time to get dressed for dinner.

4—Southern Hospitality

Dressed in a clean pair of jeans and a blouse, I went to the dining room because it was too early for the bar. I had no intention of starting the habit of drinking alcohol at 5:30 in the afternoon.

I didn't see anyone I knew at all. Eventually a waiter came and took my order, and I sat back to read my book in peace. Before my food arrived, a bellhop brought a message for me to the table. The message was from Ray to say that he would meet me in the lobby at 6:00 p.m. I checked my watch and it was 5:55, so I put down my book and looked for my waiter. When I found him, I told him that I would be back to my table in five minutes.

Searching through the lobby, I saw Ray walking through the front doors at exactly 6:00. Punctual. I waved so he would notice, and he walked towards me.

"What are you doing here, Ray? There's a hurricane outside!"

"I had to meet someone here," he answered. "I'm an old hand at these. Doesn't bother me."

"Alright, considering this is my first hurricane," I replied. "I have a table in the dining room. Would you like to join me?"

"I'd be delighted to. Just a minute though, as I said, I'm meeting someone here. I have to make a phone call first."

I returned to the table as Ray walked off to one of those alcoves to make his call. When he got to the table, my food had arrived. I motioned the waiter over again, and when he got there he scowled slightly at Ray, and then his expression cleared.

"What can I get for you, sir?" he asked.

"I'll have whatever my dinner companion is having, thank you," Ray replied.

"Very good, sir. And to drink?"

"Please bring me a gin and tonic, light on the tonic," said Ray.

The waiter left with the order, and I sipped my glass of wine.

"So I understand that you know our client?" asked Ray.

"Who do you mean?" I asked. When you're a consultant, you often end up in these three-way clients situations. My actual client is the engineering firm Ray works for. Their project is for a different company. Ultimately, that company is *the* client, and Ray is *my* client.

"I mean Mark Chisholm," said Ray.

"What does he have to do with it? I met him last Christmas. I didn't know he was the client though. At least not until he told me a month ago," I said. "Why? Is there a problem?"

"I don't think so," said Ray. "From what I understand, his company purchased the cement plant we are working for. But if it gets awkward somehow, I don't want it compromising the project, y'hear?"

"How would it get awkward?" I asked.

"How did you and Mr. Chisholm meet?" I noticed the *Mister*.

"We met in New York when I was stranded by the weather. When I went home to Montreal, I thought I would never see him again. Three months later he showed up in Montreal and we spent a couple of days together and then he left for Texas. The next thing I know, I'm in Atlanta, Georgia, starting a new project, and he surprises me at dinner on my first week."

"Do you think if he comes back here and finds you sitting with other men, that will be a problem?" asked Ray.

"What exactly do you mean 'sitting with other men?'" I answered him.

"Dating other men."

"But I'm not dating anyone."

"That's good, because I want you to have dinner with a friend of mine," said Ray. "Consider it a favor."

"Ray, I'm not comfortable with this line of conversation," I said.

"He's visiting the city, and a pretty girl like you would have a fine evening going out to dinner with him. That's all."

"Why can't he find his own date, Ray?"

"He's not from around here, and I promised him some Southern hospitality," said Ray. "He's harmless, I promise. And he's rich. So the restaurant will be top notch. Go on, you'll have fun."

Ah, so this is what all this was about. He wants me to entertain a client that isn't Mark. "Alright, but only dinner, Ray. I'm not going anywhere else with this guy. So, if he asks, the answer is no. Got it?"

"Splendid! He'll be here on Thursday. When you come into the office I'll introduce you. Now, I've got a date myself, so I must leave you for the evening."

"Well, thank you for joining me for dinner. I hope you're not going out with Caroline?" I asked.

"Why should that be a problem?" he asked wickedly.

"You know very well. You'll get that poor stupid girl's hopes up that you will marry her. She already believes she has you wrapped around her little finger. You should see the lingerie she shows off to the other girls in the office from her lunchtime shopping sprees!"

"Well now, if everyone else is seeing the wrapping before me, that's not quite fair. Perhaps I should go pick out my own wrapping?"

"Oh, you're terrible!" But I laughed at him.

With that, he departed leaving me to my thoughts and my dessert. I wanted to turn back to my book, but I found myself distracted by my musings.

How was I going to handle this friend of his? Conservatively, that's how. And I'd better be on my guard too.

After dinner, I decided to check out the bar next door. It was a fairly typical hotel bar, intimate and cozy feeling but big. There was a stage and dance floor, so I was hopeful for some entertainment. I found a table off to the side that was comfortable and took a seat. I hadn't finished my bottle of wine from dinner, so I had brought it with me. A new server came and asked me if I wanted anything to munch on, and I said perhaps later that I had just finished dinner.

"Hey, will there be a band tonight?" I asked.

"Yes, they come on at 9:00. They're here Tuesday through Friday. There is usually a special guest band on Saturdays," she answered. "Oh, by the way, my name is Janet, in case you need anything. I'm filling in for Janelle this evening."

"Hi Janet, my name is Falon," I told her. "I'll let you know."

The band came on about half an hour later. They turned out to be a rockabilly band, extremely fun music to listen to and dance to, with a mixture of Southern blues, jazz, and rock. Unfortunately, there were no other people in the bar other than a few businessmen and myself, and the staff of course. I nearly asked Janelle if she would dance with me.

At ten, the band took their first break. Most of them disappeared through a stage door, but one of them approached me where I was sitting. He walked past me to the bar, spoke to Janelle, then turned around and came and sat at my table.

"Hello there. My name is Brandon," he said.

"Hello Brandon, my name is Falon," I said, "Would you like to join me?"

"I was hoping to," he admitted. "We don't usually have an audience, so it's nice to see a pretty face in the crowd."

I smiled. "My, aren't we the flatterer?"

"I am a Southern gentleman after all, ma'am—at your service," he said with a bow and a smile.

"And just what services do you offer?" I flirted back.

"Well now, ma'am, there are too many to list at this early stage of our acquaintance," he grinned, "but I believe we can negotiate on price."

"Price?" I asked, not quite following his gist.

"Well, the price for a dance is a kiss, for example," he answered without any guile whatsoever.

"Oh, I see. That price," and in my best Southern girl accent I replied: "Well, I do declare, Mr. Brandon, you've gone a trifle too far!" I teased him.

"I'm sorry to have offended, Miss Falon. May I have this dance?"

I only just heard that the music was back and loud enough to dance to. So I offered him my hand and we got up to twirl around the floor for a while. After a few minutes I noticed this guy could dance. He had me twirling and doing a two-step, and even a jive.

We sat down five songs later, very winded and thirsty, but my wine was finished. Quickly, Janet appeared to take an order for additional beverages.

"I'd like to order some more of whatever the lady's drinking," said Brandon, "and put it on my tab please."

"That's not necessary, Brandon," I objected.

"No, but Southern gentlemen don't let a lady pay." He smiled. "I'd like a beer, please."

"Right away," said Janet.

"Thank you, Brandon."

"No problem. Wouldn't want you to go away because of thirst, now would I?"

Chatting with him was easy. When the band came back, he had to return to the stage. I sat there with more interest now that I knew one of them a little. The guys were slapping and punching Brandon on the shoulder—probably because he made contact with the only girl in the audience.

By the time they were warmed up, I noticed there were a few more people in the bar. An audience was growing, albeit mostly businessmen. It was a Thursday night, but you never knew what social habits a city has.

Janet finally had more customers to serve, so she was scurrying this way and that, carrying food and drinks back and forth from the kitchen and the bar. A couple of times she stopped at my table and asked how things were going.

The band's second set lasted until 11:00. Brandon came over to my table again and brought some of the other members. He introduced me to them all and they sat around and chatted and joked with each other. When one of them asked me to dance, I begged off saying I had to go get some sleep.

"But I'm here for a long while, so I'll see all of you tomorrow, okay?" I offered.

"*Y'all*, Falon, it's *y'all*," Brandon jested, "If you're going to be in the South, you've got to learn to speak properly!" he teased.

"I'll see y'all tomorrow, then!" That drew some smiles as the guys said goodnight to me. Laughing, I gave Janet my room number for my tab and started to leave the bar. Brandon was a sweetheart and caught up to me to walk me to the elevator. I would have to see more of him!

5—Advice from Lora

Up in my room and fresh from a good evening out, I felt the need to talk to my best friend. Checking my watch, it wasn't too late to call. Lora was usually up till 1:00 or 2:00 a.m.

"Hello," said Lora.

"Lora, it's me, I've thought about your advice," I said.

"And?"

"I agree with you, I need to date more men."

"Good for you. Any prospects?"

"Met one tonight. His name is Brandon and he is the keyboardist in a rockabilly band. They are playing at the hotel during the week, and they're really good too!"

"Oh that sounds like fun. Keyboardist, eh? Sounds like he'd be good with his fingers."

"Lora!" I groaned.

"So when will you see him?"

"I don't know, perhaps tomorrow."

"How are you feeling about Mark?"

"Better about moving on, for sure."

"Tell me, since he's Zisis, did he do that thing too?"

"What thing, oh the bite? Yeah."

"I still find it kind of weird."

"Me too, but what happens after is amazing."

"What does it feel like?"

"I cannot describe it. It's sort of like an out-of-body experience."

"Hmmm, I can relate. Some of my rituals do that to me," said Lora.

"What really drove it home was him walking into the bathroom and coming out a second later as Zisis!"

"Oh my goddess," she said quietly. "You're not kidding, are you?"

"No, I'm dead serious."

"What happened next?"

"He came clean on the truth. I just sat there and listened, getting more furious by the second. When he finished, I was stone cold furious, and knew that I would not be able to be rational, so I threw him out."

"Wait, you've skipped over the answer," said Lora. "Go back to the truth he told you. What was that?"

"He told me basically the same thing he told me five years ago when he left the first time. He added that he had to take on a new identity. They have to every ten years or so. When he saw me in New York, he said he couldn't help himself, he had to speak to me, but he did so as Mark, and didn't tell me he was Zisis. He had changed his identity."

"Oh my," said Lora quietly. "How have you left it?"

"I haven't spoken to him since."

"Have you heard from him?"

"Nope," I said. "I didn't want to hear from him until I had figured out what I wanted."

"Tell you what, go sow some oats to flush out the questions. Have your fields plowed."

Lora was making a snarfling sound on the phone as she tried not to laugh at her own joke.

"Thanks, Lora. I really appreciate your point of view."

"Bye, love, take care of yourself. And have fun!"

6—Wardrobe Update

The hurricane passed over a few days later, so that meant we could use the pool on the roof again. Since it was a Friday night, and the weather was getting hot, I decided to check out the hotel pool. Not having one of my own, this was a luxury. I hadn't brought a swimsuit with me; I hadn't known the hotel had a pool before I came down. I had meant to grab a suit the last time I went home, but I forgot.

I was also learning that the clothes I brought down with me were not lightweight enough for the South. Even though they were for spring/summer in Montreal, they were still too warm to wear here. I needed to go shopping for some more summer clothes and a swimsuit. Since I had a fairly large room, there was plenty of space for keeping clothes. This time around, the hotel was letting me keep the same room from week to week.

I stopped at the front desk.

"Excuse me, can you tell me where I can find a mall or shopping center?"

"Of course, Ms Robertson," said the concierge. He pulled out a map of the local area and drew directions on it and gave it to me.

"There is a shopping center a few blocks away from here. Follow this road to the end, and turn here, and then here," he said, pointing to the map. "They sell everything there," he added.

"Wonderful, thank you."

I left to get my rental car, drove to the mall and spent some quality time looking around. I found everything I needed and then some. Not only did I find a swimsuit, but shorts and t-shirts as well as a beach towel and underwear too. When you cannot do laundry, it's often easier to just buy new clothes.

I got back to the hotel by 7:00 p.m., hungry, so instead of going to the pool I got dressed for dinner. This time, I put on a short red skirt and a black lace top.

The maître d' looked me up and down a couple of times. After being here a month, I thought I'd met most of the desk staff at the hotel, but not this one. He started leading me to a table I didn't usually sit at.

"Excuse me, can I sit over there?" I asked, pointing to "my" table. It was in a quiet corner with good light and I liked sitting there.

"Oh, of course." He changed directions and put a menu in front of me.

"Oh that's okay, I've pretty much got it memorized."

"Have you been here for long?"

"About a month now. I'm not a usual guest. I'll be here for another five months."

"Ah! We'll have lots of time to get to know each other then."

"Indeed," I answered. Everyone was very friendly here, it seemed.

I ordered the salmon for dinner, and my favorite wine: White Zinfandel. After dinner I went back to the bar, and sure enough the same cast of characters were there again. Janelle waved me to my table and brought over the remainder of my wine from dinner again. She told me the same band was booked here for at least a month, and the boys should be in soon. Being a Friday night, the hotel bar was already starting to fill. They would have a good crowd.

Just like the last time I was here, Brandon and the other band members came and sat at my table during their break. Someone ordered shooters and beer, and soon everyone was enjoying themselves. I danced with a few of them as a group, until another guest in the bar came up to our table and asked one of the guys if he'd like to dance with her. He looked at me, then shrugged and got up to dance.

Janelle frequented our table too and soon we seemed to have a little clique going on. It seemed as though I was accepted as a member of the group by the other patrons in the hotel. When the guys got back up to play, a couple of men came over to my table to talk to me—one at a time, of course. This was different for me, as I usually didn't attract any attention at home. Maybe it was because I was Canadian and my accent was exotic down here.

At the end of the second set, the band came back to the table, and my gentlemen visitors went poof!

"Hey, Janelle, could we please order a round of shooters for the table?" asked Brandon.

"Sure, hon, I'll get them right over to you."

Sure enough, a tray of shooters showed up in a few minutes.

"Janelle...?" I started before she could whisk away.

"Yes?"

"Do you know how long the pool stays open and the bar with it?"

"The pool never closes except for storms, and the pool-bar is open till 4:00 a.m.," she answered.

"Thanks!"

"Falon, would you be interested in a midnight swim with me after the last set at 1:00 a.m.?" asked Brandon.

"That would be nice," I said. "Although I'll have to go get changed first."

"No problem, I can meet you up there."

After the last set, I signaled to Brandon that I was going to leave. He motioned up with his hand to ask about the pool, and I motioned back yes. He was getting the band's equipment packed up.

I went up to my room, changed into my new suit, grabbed my new towel, and headed on up to the pool.

When I got to the pool and walked out on deck, all the lights across the city sparkled like diamonds—and the stars, they were spectacular. *Wow!* There was no other building higher, so the pool was completely private. The deck was decorated with palm trees and planters of flowers I hadn't seen when I was up here last. The whole rooftop was lit up with lights strung from cabana to cabana and up the trunks of the trees. The bar was done up like a tiki hut, and again wrapped in lights. It was a magical place.

There were a few people enjoying a midnight swim in the pool already. A couple was swimming leisurely and playing in the water while one guy was vigorously doing lengths. I also noted there were two hot tubs tucked away in two of the corners nicely camouflaged with greenery and made slightly private as a result. There didn't seem to be anyone in either at the moment.

I walked over to the bar and took a stool.

"Good evening. What can I get you?" asked the barkeep.

"Could I please have a Scarlett O'Hara? It's a cocktail made with Southern Comfort, lime, and cranberry juice I tried a day ago, and it was delicious."

"Certainly. I can bring your order to wherever you want to sit."

"Oh, that's nice of you. Let me see, I'll put my things over by that hot tub on the left."

"Very good, miss."

I walked over to the table and chairs situated close to the hot tub, and dropped my towel and cover up on the chaise. When I walked to the stairs to get into the tub, I discovered Brandon was already there in the tub. The water was vigorously bubbling and steamy.

I could see he had brought some refreshment too. There were some bottles of beer sitting in a champagne bucket covered with ice beside the tub. He was stretched out in the water and the turbidity caused by the bubbles screened him from view. I stepped down into the hot water and a sigh escaped my lips.

"Oh, that feels amazing."

"Yes, it does," he answered. "Come all the way in, the water is great."

As I got lower into the tub, I saw he was naked. Very interesting. I should have expected that, but so what. This could be fun.

"Uh, so you forgot your suit?" I asked.

"Nah, I just prefer skinny dipping," he answered. *Good answer!*

"I didn't know the rules down here, so I dressed for the occasion," I said. "I hope you like it. Just got it today."

He looked me up and down, appraising me. There was a decidedly mischievous look in his eyes.

"I love the bathing suit," he grinned.

The sensation of stepping into the steaming water was wonderful. I could feel layers of tension and exhaustion melting away. I wasn't particularly tense or tired, but when you get into hot water like this, it always relaxes you more.

I slid under the surface and held myself completely submerged for a few moments. When I came up for air, Brandon was a little closer to me and he was sitting up.

"Miss, here is your cocktail, would you like it on the side of the tub?" asked the barkeep who had just brought my drink.

"Please, right here would be wonderful."

He had a special tray with him that hooked onto the side of the hot tub, and put my glass along with some snacks on it, then walked away.

"That's great service," I said.

"We try to go the extra mile in the South," said Brandon. "May I offer you a backrub?"

"Mmmm, that would be nice. Do you know how to massage?" I asked.

"I'm told I'm pretty good," he said.

I turned around so my back was toward him and sat cross-legged in the water. He started at my neck, working his way across my shoulders and down my back. I was wearing a one-piece suit because it was practical for swimming, and I thought I looked better in a one-piece suit. This one-piece had a very low back and a low neckline with a zipper in the front. The zipper was more decorative than anything, but it did unzip provocatively low.

As Brandon worked his fingers down my back, I waited in anticipation to see if he would be overt. His hands felt great working over my back. He was making his way lower and lower.

I considered what I would do if he made a move. Considering my conversation with Lora, I was thinking I should have some fun. He was a nice-looking man, with a fit, firm body. He was interesting and well-spoken, and we had fun together. I decided that I would enjoy myself.

Brandon continued to massage my back, then shifted away from me after behaving like the perfect gentleman. Did I feel disappointment? He had moved over to the far side of the hot tub again and was stretched out in the water. I could tell he had his legs crossed over at the ankles and was preventing himself from floating, which was a bit tricky in the bubble streams of the jets.

Hmmm, is he playing a coy game or is he not interested? Nah, he wouldn't have come here naked if he wasn't interested. So this is a game. Okay, Mr. Brandon, I'll play.

"Are you enjoying Atlanta?" he said, trying to sound casual.

"Mmmm, yes, I am. Although I haven't seen much of it yet." I raised my glass and took a gulp of my cocktail. Hot water makes you thirsty!

"I did a little shopping after work, but I'm still feeling my way around at the office and trying not to get lost!" I replied. I took another large gulp of my drink. It was now finished, and my head was getting just a little light.

"That's good. I can show you some of the city if you're interested. I'm from Atlanta, even though I tend to be on the road more often than not with the band. It's nice to be home for a change," he said. "Barkeep, could we please have another round?" he called over to the bar.

"Sightseeing would be nice. I've read some history of the city and it's pretty interesting," I responded. "Thank you," I said to the waiter as he placed another glass on my tray.

"I was thinking more of the social life here. You see, many of the counties around the city are dry, so it works a bit differently here. You may have noticed that the city basically empties at five."

"So I've heard. I asked the concierge about that on my second day here. I had been invited to a colleague's home, but I didn't know them at all. It's an interesting social tradition."

"There aren't many clubs or such downtown. They're in the outlying areas. Atlanta has become a city of transferred people, with the increasing number of head offices being set up here. It's great for the city, but it creates a separate social structure," he explained. "The downtown core basically empties at five as everyone goes home. It's bad for the restaurants and many of the businesses that survive on tourism. Many of the transferees don't understand that the surrounding bedroom communities are dry when they get here, so they party in their homes."

"My colleagues keep asking me to go to their homes after work. In Montreal, you don't usually do that unless you're good friends. I don't know these people, so it felt a little strange."

"It's a Southern courtesy. If you're gonna be drinkin', invite everyone!"

As we were talking, Brandon had relaxed and was moving closer, a little bit at a time. Eventually, he was on the seat next to mine and he had his arms stretched out along the top of the tub. He was carefully keeping himself in the jet streams so the bubbles would flow fully around him, masking his body.

The anticipation was killing me. I could feel butterflies taking flight in my stomach.

The naughty side of me was dying of curiosity. So I sidled right up to him and put my hands under the water. He was watching me closely. I was submerged to just over my breasts, but you saw ample cleavage. I reached up and slowly started pulling down my zipper.

I glanced up and looked in his eyes. They were a warm caramel color—like that of a soft toffee. I was watching his face as I pulled on my zipper. The irises expanded ever so slightly as his excitement increased. I stopped pulling just under my breasts. The result was they were trying to spill free of the suit but were still well contained. Abundantly visible.

"It's nice being here with you," said Brandon softly. His voice caught a titch.

"Yes, it is," I leaned over and kissed him lightly on the lips. His hand moved up and cupped one of my breasts and it dripped over him. When I pulled away a little after the kiss, his other hand went behind my back.

"Don't move away," he said.

I shifted myself closer and turned toward him. He picked me up and put me on his lap so I was facing him. Then he pulled me in for a kiss. It was tentative at first, then it became hungry as his lips opened and his tongue darted out. I opened my mouth to him and let him explore.

The kiss became more ardent, and he wrapped his arms around me, with his hands exploring my body. They traveled down my suit and into the back to grab my ass as well as taking my breasts and playing with the nipples.

All the while his mouth was hungrily consuming mine. A delightful bulge was making itself known between my hip and his body. I took my hand that wasn't doing much and grasped it around.

His gasp sent tingles down my neck because we were still kissing. I pulled my leg across him so that I was straddling his lap now. Good thing the bench was deep; there was a place for my feet to go. I was stroking his shaft with one hand when I decided to slip it inside my suit.

However, Brandon had another idea. He had pulled the zipper down completely, and that meant my suit could come off easily. I pushed off from him, separating us just enough to slip a shoulder strap off. He got the idea and followed me to the deeper part of the tub and slipped the other shoulder off. His hands worked the suit down my body, pausing at my breasts, cupping them together and burying his face between them. When my suit was down to my hips, he slipped his hands inside and pushed down past my ass. Then his hands came back up and cupped my ass and my mound at once. I kicked off the suit.

I was floating vertically in the tub with my legs bent at the knee when Brandon came over and wrapped his arms around me. His shaft pushed between my legs, telling me he wanted to play too. I took his shaft and rubbed it between my legs.

"Ahh, that feels amazing," he said. "You're a real turn-on."

Lifting one of my legs slightly let me angle myself so that I could place his shaft at my opening. When I did so, he twitched excitedly. So I rubbed him back and forth along my slit.

"Woman, I want in," he growled at me. Then he pulled me over to the shallow side of the tub, pushing me up against the wall so that he could penetrate me.

"Oh, you're so tight, I love it," he murmured. As he started to move in and out, I added a finger to my vagina.

"Oh, like that, hmmm?" He added his own fingers to my vagina too, making it feel really tight. I groaned in pleasure as his fingers found one of my g-spots inside. His thumb was trying to stimulate my clit, but not quite getting it.

Brandon started to move faster, and his shaft engorged a little until he was nearly at the point of climax. I pulled away from him quickly, forcing him to pull out.

"What the…?" he cried.

"Shhhh, watch," I said. I turned around so that my back was to him and kneeled on the platform underwater. My ass was up in the air. "Take me this way."

He grabbed my ass and moved himself around me and played with my slit a bit. When he positioned his cock at my vagina it was a little softer, but it would do the trick. He pushed in slowly until he was completely buried inside me.

"Oh fuck! That feels good. God, you're a deep woman. You've taken my whole cock."

"I knew you would like this position."

Brandon started thrusting himself hard. With the added traction, he could really penetrate me as completely as he could. Not all the way for me. He started slowly, hard but slow. As he lost control, he sped up until he was really pounding me. When he came, the climax was forceful but not very long.

He stayed connected to me for a few seconds, collecting his breath, and then it seemed like he suddenly remembered there was another person doing this with him.

"Falon, that was fun. How are you doing?"

For me it was like riding like a horse, exciting and fun but without an emotional connection. It was short, though. I'm used to a longer session.

"It was fun, yes," I agreed with him.

His cock had shrunk to the point that he pulled out of me and sat back down in the water. I moved and sat beside him. The hot tub water swirled away some of the cum that was leaking out. I took my hand and made sure the folds of my skin were rinsed in the water too.

He reached for my hand and pulled me back. He looked at me and smiled. "You are very sexy, you know?"

"Mmmm, thank you," I answered.

"Well, you are a complete turn-on. That bathing suit is amazing. I like your body and its curves."

Not really knowing what to say, I grabbed my swimsuit. "Help me put it back on?" I asked him.

"Absolutely, that could be just as fun," he added.

As I lay there in the water, he helped me put the suit back on by sliding it up my legs, with his hand slowly reaching for my core and tickling me lightly. He slipped a finger or two inside as the suit settled in place, and rubbed my g-spot. Heat started generating inside me again as a little gasp escaped my lips. He smiled as he withdrew his fingers and continued pulling my suit over my hips and then the straps over my shoulders, leaving my breasts hanging out.

His finger went down my suit from the bottom of the zipper, rubbing my nub until I was gasping again. He started kissing and nipping and sucking me up the length of the zipper until he got to my breasts. He pushed them together and massaged them, roughly licking the hard nipples and sucking on them until they hurt from excitement. He pulled my shoulders up so I wasn't sitting in deep water and pushed his cock between my breasts. His eyes almost crossed as he pushed himself up and down between my breasts.

I caught his penis in my hands on his upstroke and bent down and sucked his head with my lips.

"Oh, oh, oh, geez, ah—I, I, oh my! I cannot hold it."

Then he was ejaculating again as his sperm erupted into my mouth.

"Oh, sorry, I didn't mean that to happen!"

Brandon was soft now, and I took a moment to again rinse off my face and rinse out my mouth a little. He moved over to me and sexily pulled up my zipper so that my suit was fully on now.

"Um, that was amazing. Thank you," he said. "I really hadn't expected that at all."

"Thanks for the shag," I replied glibly. Then I got out of the tub, downed the rest of my drink, wrapped my towel around my body, and went back to my room to have a shower to clean off.

Remind me to not use that hot tub for a few days!

It was sort of fun. But he was no Mark. So what did I learn? There were lots of ways to have sex, and lots of degrees of competency. I needed a larger sample if we're to make any really accurate and meaningful determinations.

7—The Morning After

I felt like death warmed over this morning after partying with Brandon.

To make matters worse, my mom called this morning at 9:00! It took all the strength I had to reach out of my deep sleep to get the phone. Of course I couldn't let her know that I was partying with "strange" men. I had to pretend that my life was boring and nothing was happening.

She felt safe that way. My mom worried about me constantly, or at least she said she did. If she knew for a fact I was behaving like an adult, she'd probably have a conniption fit. As it was, I let her believe I was being a boring "good" girl and not having any fun. That way I was safe.

Okay, I was vertical—barely. I couldn't go to the kitchen to get coffee in my PJ's—or naked either. I had to get dressed and that meant a shower.

Ugh! Coffee ... coffee ... I need coffee...

I stumbled into the living room and made a pot of coffee with the tiny hotel coffee maker, then went and got into the shower. After letting the water sluice over me for ten minutes, I started to wake up.

My initial thought was about Brandon and what we did last night. It hadn't been earth-quaking, toe-curling, "I wanna have your baby and let's get started right now" sex. The connection between us was stronger across a table than in the throes of lustful passion. That meant something. I wasn't sure what yet.

If I compared him to Mark or Zisis—there was no comparison.

I was going to put that out of my mind and do things for myself this weekend. I needed a change of pace, something physical to put my thoughts in the back of my brain so it could sort through all of this in the background.

More shopping was called for. I needed to try on more clothes and men as well, see which ones fit best. The coffee was waking me up, and a few Motrin tablets were making me feel better. I finished getting dressed, drank some more of the room coffee—*ugh, terrible stuff*—and headed off to the restaurant. I didn't know what to do today, so I decided to check at the front desk and find out if there was a movie theater close by and what else there was to do in the neighborhood.

"Good morning, can you tell me where the nearest movie theater is?"

"Certainly, Ms. Robertson. There is another shopping mall about three miles from here at the end of Peachtree Boulevard. There is a six-screen theater there."

"Perfect!"

"Oh, and Ms Robertson, just to let you know, we have a special band with us tonight—the Tom Cats are with us."

"Oh really? They're one of my favorite bands! Thanks for telling me. Does that mean the regular guys aren't here?"

"They take weekends off. They'll be back on Monday."

"Good to know." That was actually perfect. It meant I wouldn't be running into Brandon.

Armed with that information, I grabbed a newspaper and went to have breakfast. The dining room was pretty full this morning with more tourists than businesspeople, so I didn't get my "usual" table.

I spent a leisurely hour having breakfast and reading the paper with real coffee. By the time I was finished, it was nearly noon, so I looked up the movies playing in town and their times. Perhaps I would go do some book shopping so I had reading material at hand for the afternoon. There was also the pool up on the roof, but I thought it might be a little too hot up there to go swimming. Still, before I left the hotel, I went and checked the pool to see how busy it was.

Sure enough, there were a few parents and lots of kids splashing around and having a great time. It was hot up there, but I was surprised at the wind that was blowing across the pool deck. It felt cooler than I had expected. I spotted a number of people in the hot tub and remembered what it had been used for last night.

Gosh, I hope they use lots of chlorine!

There were two couples in the hot tub now, sitting close together and talking with drinks in their hands. Were they planning something for later too?

Coming back to the pool later this evening was a good possibility. I set out to find the bookstore and the theater. It was a pleasant afternoon. The sun was out; it was hot and humid, but there was a breeze that helped keep the air moving. Atlanta can get really sultry in the summer.

The streets were lined with peach trees—they were everywhere. And the air smelled like canned peaches. A lot of the street names had "peach" in them, like Peach Tree Lane or Peach Basket Drive. It was going to make navigating a little tricky. So I decided to go in a straight line. Thankfully, the hotel was on a main street, and that went through a fairly large commercial area. Peachtree Boulevard intersected the street the hotel was on, and the mall was on the corner.

The mall was large, complete with a Saks Fifth Avenue store and a huge bookstore. Inside, the air conditioning was on full blast, and it was cool and inviting. There weren't many places in the South that weren't air conditioned. The stores were bright and there were some different ones I hadn't seen before, so it was interesting to see what was there. I did a complete tour of the mall first to familiarize myself with the layout. It was designed like any mall at home. However, they had a water park in the middle; not a big one, but it was kind of cool. Of course, it was filled with children, and mostly dads while the moms were off shopping.

I grabbed myself an ice cream and went to sit down on a bench to watch the fun at the water park. A guy came and sat down beside me on the same bench and had a pile of shopping bags with him. I glanced at the bags and noticed they were mostly from clothing stores, and some of them kids stores. I figured he was a dad waiting on his kids and wife.

When I got up to leave, I decided my first stop would be the gigantic bookstore I had found at one end of the mall. I had walked about seven meters when someone gently touched my shoulder and I turned around. It was the guy who had sat down beside me on the bench.

"Yes? Can I help you?" I asked.

"Did you drop this?" he asked, holding out a bag.

"No, but thanks for asking," I answered, glancing down at what was in his hand. "Didn't I see you carrying that when you sat down?"

"Um, yes, I was," he admitted, "but I couldn't think of anything else to say to stop you."

Do all gentlemen of the South have this much guile? I asked myself.

"Hello would have done," I countered. Then I turned around and continued to walk down the mall. He caught up with me again and touched me on the shoulder a second time.

"Hello, my name is Rick. Can I buy you a coffee?"

"Hello, Rick, I'm Falon," I answered.

"How 'bout that coffee?" he asked again.

I looked at him and narrowed my eyes, carefully assessing the situation. I decided I would not let him know who I really was, or where I was staying. But a cup of coffee and some conversation would be nice. After all, you can't make friends if you don't talk to people.

"Where would we go?" I asked.

"There's a coffee shop that serves nice pastries just down the mall that way," he answered, pointing the way I was walking.

I glanced at his left hand again, wondering if there was a ring; there was none. Apparently, that didn't mean anything, because he was definitely carrying children's clothes.

"Won't your wife and family be wondering where you are?" I asked pointedly, looking at his bags.

"Ah, these aren't for my kids. I'm buying clothes and toys for a charity. I'm not actually married."

Well, he's either an extremely creative liar or the real deal.

"Alright, but I have plans for later this afternoon. I'm meeting a friend at the movies," I lied. There was no reason to leave myself open completely.

So off we went, him leading the way through the crowds to the coffee shop that happened to be next door to the bookstore. *How convenient. Perhaps I could persuade him to shop for books? That would give me an indication of what kind of personality he had.*

"So, Rick, do you come here often?" I asked with a smirk. "You said your parcels are for charity?"

"Yes, I regularly help out a charity that collects food, toys, and clothes for children to distribute in time for school. Many kids in Atlanta don't get proper breakfasts or clothes, and they go to school hungry. So I have set up a charity that feeds them breakfast and gives them clean clothes before school.

Sometimes, it's the only meal they get that day. Often the kids can be seen wearing the same clothes many days in a row too, because it's the only thing they have."

"As you see, I'm quite passionate about this. So, yes, actually I do come here often," he said. "I don't live too far away, but I work close by."

"Oh? What do you do for a living?"

"I cook."

"You're a chef?"

"Not yet, a sous-chef at the moment."

"Commercial, restaurant?"

"Restaurant. It's a steakhouse. What do you do? You're not from around here judging by your accent."

"No, I'm Canadian. I'm here for a six-month contract. I develop software education."

"Oh that sounds exciting."

"Not really. It's pretty pedantic actually. I liaise between the end users and the programmers. There is never a meeting of minds, and there are always problems. But what is interesting is the application of the software. I find it fascinating how things work."

"Do they rent you a house?"

"No, I stay in hotels. Speaking of locals, you aren't Southern either."

"No, I'm Cuban. I moved to America when I was fifteen. I haven't developed Southern accent, but I've lost most of my Cuban accent."

"Was it tough immigrating to the US? Are you here as DACA?"

"Thankfully, no. My parents were able to obtain US citizenship as a special compensation to Cuban people escaping Castro. I cannot imagine the hardship of being DACA."

"Canada doesn't have immigration laws like that. We don't 'disallow' people from applying for citizenship."

"How long are you in Atlanta? Which hotel are you in?"

"I'm staying at the Holiday Inn down the main street there. Not far from the mall actually."

"No kidding! My restaurant is next door!"

"Oh my, isn't it a small world? I'll have to stop by, then. Especially since I know the chef now."

"Sous-chef."

"Well, it's about time for me to get to the movie," I said getting up, "and I want to duck into the bookstore beforehand, so thank you for the coffee and pastry. It was a pleasure meeting you."

"Wait, can I call you at the hotel?" asked Rick.

"Sure, ask for Falon Robertson. Bye!"

We parted company, me going into the bookstore and him moving off into the crowded mall. I watched him for a minute to make sure he was leaving, then turned into the store in search of my favorite authors. I had several, and I always looked to see if their new books were out yet. One of my favorites was Jean Auel and her *Earth's Children* series; another was David Eddings, and I love Anne Rice. But I think Diana Gabaldon won the top spot. Oh, those love scenes with Jamie! All very different authors!

There was something about a bookstore I adored: the serene atmosphere, the stacks of new books. I walked through the store looking at all the covers. Some caught my attention by their artwork, others grabbed me with their titles. I love books. I had a huge collection, and my friends thought I was nuts because I refused to give any of them away. I was dangerous in a bookstore, often leaving the store with $500 or

$600 less in my wallet. I couldn't help myself. All the stories just look so interesting and compelling. It was kind of a compulsion, I suppose. I don't apologize for it. For some women, it's shoes. For me, it's books.

This trip, I brought some books with me. But they make the suitcase heavy, so I had to be judicious. It was easier to pick up books in Atlanta, but then I'd have to get them home. I didn't always have time to read while I was away. I wished I could just go sit by the pool and read all day long. Alas, I was on a business trip, not a vacation.

Not finding anything new by my favorite authors, I looked around for new titles. A great place to look, if the store has one, was the bargain table. I'd found some great first edition hardcovers on the bargain table for a couple of dollars. It was how I found David Eddings and Jean Auel. I found their first books on the bargain table and then discovered they were the beginning of a series.

Picking up three or four books that looked interesting, I walked to the front of the store to pay. There was a small lineup but it went quickly. Glancing at my watch, it was time I started for the theater, which had a connection to the mall. I should just make it on time for the movie.

I read the billboard and selected a rom-com. It was a fun flick, light entertainment for a Saturday afternoon. Relaxed, and feeling somewhat rested, I returned home to the hotel after the movie with my books. At least I would have something to distract me through dinner.

8—Rock This Town

Looking forward to the band tonight, I decided to go change before eating. As I was passing the front desk, Franco caught my attention and said there was a package waiting for me.

Puzzled, I went to the desk and picked up a soft package that only had my name on it, no other indicator of who left it. I got back to my room, I opened up the package to find it was a beach towel—a luxurious, oversized beach towel. There was a note inside the package that said, "In case you wanted another midnight swim." It was unsigned. Obviously it was from Brandon, as he was the only one who knew I went swimming last night.

After I had changed, I grabbed one of my new books and went back downstairs to eat. Half-expecting a surprise visitor, I looked around the lobby for faces I knew. I had the sensation of being watched.

Get a grip, Falon!

Sitting at my usual table, I ordered a steak dinner this time. Instead of my usual bottle of wine, I decided on a margarita. The meal was good as usual, and it was nice to get into a new book. Completely engrossed with the new story, I didn't even notice the server clearing the dishes after I was finished. She had to knock on the table to get my attention to ask about dessert and coffee.

"I'll get that," said a smooth, deep voice behind me.

I turned around to see another strange man, light and athletic looking, walking up to me.

"May I join you?" he asked me. I got a very strange vibe off him. It set my nerves on edge.

"Do I know you?" I asked.

It was starting to feel like a dating service. Didn't anyone respect the solitude of someone reading? I really didn't want company right now. I wanted to read.

"Forgive my bad manners. My name is Derek," he answered smoothly.

"Hello, Derek, I'm pleased to meet you. However, I'd rather be alone right now. I was really looking forward to starting my new book. Perhaps another time?" I answered, hoping that would put him off.

"Of course. Please excuse my intrusion," he said to me. "Please let me pay for the lady's repast," Derek said to the server.

"Ah, that is not necessary, thank you," I spoke quickly. The last thing I wanted was to be owing someone some courtesy I didn't want to repay.

"Think of it as compensation for disturbing your meal," he suggested smoothly.

What's with these Southern guys? Oh boy, I wasn't going to rid myself of this one easily. The only thing I could think of was to be gracious and coolly distant.

"Thank you, sir, for your kindness," I drawled. "But it's quite unnecessary."

He bowed, turned, and walked away. I turned to my server, who was smiling, and asked her if this happens in the South often.

"Yes, it does," she said. "I see these guys behaving like this all the time. It's kind of cute until it becomes annoying."

"No kidding!" I laughed. "You're not from here. Your accent is barely a drawl. Where are you from?"

"You're quite right. I'm from Harlem, New York. I got out when I got a scholarship to university."

"Hi, fellow Northerner, I'm Falon!"

"Hi there, Falon. I'm Charity. Yes, it's a nickname, because my brothers always teased me that I was a charity case!" She laughed. "The name stuck and it became fashionable."

"What brought you down to Georgia?" I enquired.

"Well, this hotel chain believes in moving their staff around the country so they can learn new cultures and how to deal with different people. For a black, female, New Yorker, they felt that a stint in Georgia would give me insight."

"In what way?" I asked.

"I don't know. What did I learn was that here in the south, racism is just more out in the open. I already know how to deal with that shit. We learn from a very young age."

"It makes me feel ill to hear how they treat other people!" I said. "Someone actually used the n-word toward another member of the wait staff yesterday. I was flabbergasted."

"It makes you sick? Imagine being on the receiving end!"

"I can't. I can only sympathize. I'll never know the level of racism you have to deal with daily."

"Well, I'll see you later, okay?"

"Later!" I was missing girl time since I didn't have Lora our party nights together. I must call her tomorrow and see how she was. *And Armand too, to see how the boys were doing without me.*

Returning to my book, I was soon lost in the story. I didn't notice that the dining room had become quite full until the maître d' came up to me and asked me if I could give up my table for the night. Apologizing, I scooped up my book and bag and went into the bar. There was a good crowd tonight, and Charity was serving in there too. She motioned me to a table in the back she was serving.

The Tom Cats had started their show and they were cooking. Great music, great sound, and soon I found myself chair dancing—what I call bopping around in my seat. They were playing some of my favorite songs and I knew the words to them. I had been listening to them since 1982 when I first heard the *Tom Cat Crawl*. I loved that song so much, I had memorized all the words. So, I packed up my book and made my way to the bar. I didn't want to miss them live.

When the Tom Cats started playing *Tom Cat Crawl*, I couldn't help myself and I got up to dance alone. I moved close to the stage and was bopping along to the music. There were quite a few people on the dance floor already, and some of them started dancing along with me.

I was having a ball. The margaritas must have helped me lose my inhibitions, because I started to cut loose and dance the way Lora and I danced when we went out together. Eventually, the people who tried partnering me gave up and moved back because they couldn't keep up. A small clearing appeared around me as I got further into the music.

It was only when I noticed the lead singer was watching me closely that I saw I was by myself and that everyone was watching me. One person had a video camera pointed at me. *Oh my.* I suppose it must have looked like I was an exhibitionist.

The next song was Brian Setzer's *Rock This Town,* and that sent me into the stratosphere. I heard everyone clapping to the music along with me now, and the band was smiling because I had obviously charged the room up. Everyone was dancing and singing along to the music. Someone came over to me and grabbed my hand and flung me into a jive dance. The two of us twirled and kicked our way around the stage, while everyone stood back and watched.

At the end of the set, I was so hot and sweaty I begged off and returned to my table. To my surprise, the lead singer came over to thank me for the help.

"Help?" I asked.

"The room was kind of slow until you entered and started dancing. So thank you for getting everyone up on the floor!" he said.

"Oh, hey, I love your music. I've been a big fan for almost twenty years. I remember hearing *Tom Cat Crawl* for the first time, and my friends and I would be skiing and singing it at the top of our lungs all the way down the mountain!"

"Skiing? Where are you from?" he asked.

"Montreal, Canada," I said.

"Wow, that's a long way from here. What brings you to the deep South?" he asked. "By the way, my name is Bobby Styles."

"I know," I blushed. "My name is Falon. It's a real honor to meet you."

"Hey, it's an honor for me to meet a big fan!" said Bobby. "So why are you in Georgia?"

"Business," I said. "I work for a software company. I'm down here developing education for software that we have installed at a client's location."

"That sounds complicated," said Bobby. "How long does that usually take?"

"Oh, anywhere from four to six months usually. It's a lengthy process."

"And you'll be in Georgia the whole time? What about family?" he asked.

"Not being married helps," I said. "It's one of the reasons I got the job. I was free to travel for the company. A neighbor takes care of my cats at home, and I return every other weekend to exchange clothes and do laundry."

"Do you mind if I join you for the break?" asked Bobby.

"No, please have a seat. I'm waiting for Charity until she's off, then we're going out. But until then I'd love to talk to you!"

"You won't be staying for the whole show?" He almost looked disappointed.

"When do you finish tonight?" I asked him.

Ooops! I just realized what that question would sound like. It's a good thing it was dark in the bar because I was blushing again.

"I'm off at about 2:00, and then the roadies take over and pack up the equipment," he said. There was a smirk on his face.

"I am not sure how long it will be until she's finished work," I pondered out loud, "but I'm here until then. Aren't you here again tomorrow night?" I asked hopefully.

"No, we're on the road again to Miami tomorrow. We have a gig down there for a couple of weeks. This was a paid stop, so to speak."

"Oh." I was clearly disappointed. One of my favorite bands and I was going to miss most of their performance here. I wonder if Charity would mind me staying?

"I'll tell you what," Bobby started, "if you're still here after the second set, I'll come back to your table and we can talk some more. All right?"

"I would like that," I nodded. "Very much."

He left to walk behind the stage and disappeared where the rest of the band had gone. A few minutes later, Charity came over and I noticed a wide grin splitting her face.

"Soooooo, what did he have to say?" she asked me.

"Oh, he just came over to say hi and to thank me for picking up the pace of the audience," I giggled. "Can you imagine? Bobby Styles spoke to me!" I exclaimed.

"Hey, if you want, we can hang here a while. My boss said it was okay. I asked on account of the chat you and the lead act had. He noticed that you were good for the bar, you see." She was smiling broadly now. "Good for the bar! Hmmmmpf!"

We both laughed, but I was happy to get to watch the balance of the act. Charity and I were dancing the whole time, putting on quite the floor show. It turned out that she was a very good dancer too.

During both the second and third breaks, Bobby came over to chat again and spent a little time at our table before disappearing into the back of the bar.

"What is back there? A dressing room?" I asked Charity.

"Yeah, it's a dressing room, complete with washrooms and a bedroom," she responded. "Sometimes the acts 'entertain' in the back, so the hotel opened up one of the rooms to the back a couple of years ago, so they could 'discreetly' have their parties."

"I take it that it's not always so discreet?" I asked.

"Hardly. Sometimes it's downright circus-like back there," she laughed.

The entire night passed by so quickly that I couldn't believe it. I was flying high when we finally left the bar after saying goodbyes to the band. Everyone waved and spoke to us, and Bobby came and shook my hand, thanking me again. He said he loved having people to perform for like us because it makes the music come alive. I was genuinely touched.

Charity took off for her home, and I went up to my room. When I got there I remembered the beach towel I had received as a gift.

Should I go have another "midnight" swim?

9—Road Trip

Last night, I thought better of going to the pool again. I was a good girl and went to bed. Today was Sunday, so I would do some more exploring. Perhaps get some road directions to nearby tourist attractions. After all, there was no reason I couldn't be a tourist just because I was living here for six months.

For a change, I woke up refreshed. I had slept in until 10:30 and was downstairs for breakfast by 12:00. There was a wonderful brunch buffet laid out in the dining room today. That was a good thing to remember: *they serve Sunday brunch, yum.* I brought my book with me again. I planned on spending some quality time with it at breakfast.

The food smelled delicious. I helped myself to pancakes and French toast, bacon, eggs, and fruit. Breakfast is my favorite meal. I could eat it any time of the day or night. One of my most loved restaurants back home specialized in breakfast. They had turned breakfast into an art form, with delicate crêpes stuffed with anything you can imagine. Here the food was plain but flavourful, fresh, and not greasy.

Since the dining room didn't seem to be too busy, I was not rushed from my table, and got to linger until 2:00. After brunch, I walked over to the front desk and looked for area maps and attractions. Atlanta had an aquarium, which looked interesting, and the Martin Luther King Jr. Memorial site, which would be historic. Atlanta was a modern city, but it had old roots that you could see, like at the Underground. The Atlanta Botanical Gardens would be a treat too.

There were many things to do and lots of neighborhoods to poke around. I learned that the city of Savannah was only three hours away and it was right on the ocean. That might be a nice day trip, but it would have to be the next weekend when I stayed down here.

Suddenly feeling lazy, I decided to go back to my room and read some more. When I got there, that towel was egging me on to go to the pool. So I changed into my swimsuit, which was still a little damp, grabbed the towel and my book and went up to the pool to relax. That proved to be a good idea. I had the place completely to myself! I selected a chair under a gazebo in the shade and stretched out on my new towel and settled into my book.

I woke up suddenly with a tap on my shoulder. I hadn't realized I'd fallen asleep. I opened my eyes to see a waiter standing over me. I glanced at my watch. *Wow!* I had been asleep for almost two hours!

"Yes?" I asked.

"Would you like something to drink, ma'am?" he asked.

"Mmmm, that would be nice. What 'cha got?"

"Anything you like, ma'am. The bar is open now," he answered.

"I'd like a margarita then, please."

"Right away, ma'am. What is your room number?"

"It's 1023," I answered.

That was nice, drinks in the afternoon. I looked around and saw that some people had joined me on the deck and I hadn't noticed or woken up. I must have needed the extra sleep. Luckily, I was still under the shade. Otherwise, I would have gotten a terrible sunburn.

The waiter returned shortly with my drink and set it on a small table next to me. It was deliciously cold and refreshing. I sat there sipping my drink and reading my book. Again I settled into the story and was engrossed in it when a shadow crossed my pages. I stopped reading and looked up. It was not the waiter.

"Good afternoon, Falon," said Derek.

I groaned. *Not this guy again.* I had no idea how he got my name. I had not given it to him the other day.

"Good afternoon. It was Derek, correct?" I said coolly.

"May I join you?" he asked.

"I'd really rather not," I answered.

"Am I interrupting your book again?" he asked primly.

"Actually, yes. Yes, you are."

"May I take you to dinner, then? Say 7:30 this evening?" he asked in a forward way.

"I am meeting someone else, thank you," I lied.

"That is too bad. Perhaps tomorrow evening, then?"

"Derek, I am not interested in having dinner with you. Please do not ask again. Nor am I interested in having drinks with you," I stated categorically.

"There is no need to be rude," he said, getting huffy.

"Well, you were not getting the hints I dropped, so I believed you had to be told bluntly," I seethed. There was something about this guy that rubbed me the wrong way. I wasn't going to examine it. I just had an instinct about this individual. He made the hair on the back of my neck spike up and gave me the heebee-geebees. Maybe it was the freaky looking tattoo on his hand that did it.

"Very well. I shall leave you to your book. But you shall be sorry you did not take me up on my offer," he said smugly.

I didn't rise to that one! *What an ego! I shall be sorry? Huh! Go figure!* Then I remembered I had no meeting for tonight's dinner, so I'd better find one quickly. Otherwise my lack of an alibi would blow my cover, and the way this guy was persistent he'd be all over me like a wet blanket. Of course, I could just get room service. That was a thought. Ah, but I wanted to go to the bar for the music later, and I had better not go without someone. Who could I call?

There was the guy I met at the mall—he was kind of cute and shy. There was Brandon—but that would be a second date and I wasn't sure I wanted that. I could see if Charity was working tonight. I decided to take a chance and try to reach Rick, the guy from the mall. He seemed harmless and didn't have an ego. However, I wasn't going to do anything about that right now. I was comfortable with my book and my drink. It would be a terrible waste not to drink this margarita.

Around 5:00, I was starting to get hungry, so it was time to get up and go see if I could find a phone number for Rick. I put on the cover-up I purchased and grabbed my towel and my book and went down to the front desk. When I got there Franco was on duty again.

"Hi, Franco, how are you today?" I asked him.

"I'm fine, Ms. Robertson, thank you, and yourself?" he answered politely.

"I am feeling wonderful, thank you. By any chance, is there a message for me?"

"I'll check." He went to a book where they listed all the messages coming in for guests and wrote something down on a message slip and returned. "Yes, there was. A gentleman by the name of Ricardo Benal called about three hours ago and left his number for you." He handed me the slip of paper.

"Thank you, Franco. Have a nice evening, y'hear?" I smiled. I was getting into this Southern drawl thing.

Armed with the message, I went back to my room to make the call. I figured I could call from there and change quickly in case he was available.

"Hello, is Rick there, please?" I asked into the phone after a voice answered on the other end.

"Just a minute," the voice said. I couldn't tell if it was male or female, having neither a high nor a low tone.

"Hello?" came Rick's voice a few seconds later. "This is Rick."

"Hello, Rick, this is Falon," I was uncertain of the response I would get.

"Hi, Falon! I was hoping you would call back," said Rick. "Are you free tonight by any chance?"

"I was calling to ask you the same thing," I answered. "So I guess we both are!" I laughed.

"You first," he said.

"Okay, I was wondering if you would like to join me for dinner here at the hotel, and then accompany me to the bar later. They have a live blues band and a dance floor," I asked in a rush.

"I'd be happy to," he answered hesitatingly. "Although I managed to pick up some tickets to a show—music—of a band that is one of my favorites and I was hoping to ask you to come along with me," he explained.

"Oh, that sounds fun too," I answered. "Who is the band?"

"The Tom Cats," said Rick. "They're playing in Tallahassee, Florida, tonight."

"Isn't that a long drive?" I asked.

"It's only three hours. If we leave in the next half hour, we can be there in time for their first set." He sounded genuinely excited.

Three hours was a longer drive than I expected to do tonight. And it would be three hours back too at 2:00 in the morning. I won't get any sleep tonight! Oh my, but it was one of my most loved bands! *And to see Bobby's face when I am there again! He'll think I'm a groupie! Oh, what the hell!*

"Sure, it sounds fun. I really like the Tom Cats myself, and it would be a real treat to see them live again."

"Again?" asked Rick.

"They were here at the hotel last night! It's too bad I didn't know how much you liked them too or I would have invited you."

"So can I pick you up now?" he asked.

"Let me change first. It'll only take me a minute to change and be downstairs."

"I'm literally walking out the door of the restaurant. The hotel is just a few steps away. I can meet you in the lobby in two minutes," he said.

"Really? I thought I called you at home. Where was I calling?" I asked.

"The restaurant."

"Oh, good."

The elevator dinged as the car reached the lobby, and the door opened. I chuckled when I saw Rick standing there.

"Hello," I said, clearing the elevator door. "That was fast!"

Rick was looking very urban dressed in black—black jeans, black shirt, and black boots. His shirt was open to mid-chest and he had a fresh look to him like he had just stepped off a long cruise. He looked relaxed, not at all like the first time I met him. I could see his Latin roots now. He exuded Latin sensuality.

I took a closer look. His face was tanned, with high cheekbones, deep set eyes of brown, sculpted eyebrows that weren't heavy over his eyes. A long straight nose, and perfectly formed lips. He had a strong chin, but it wasn't pointy, and his jawline was strong too. His profile was quite masculine. Broad of shoulder—that I hadn't really noticed yesterday. Narrow waist and hips. Cute butt.

His clothes fit him like they were custom made. The shirt had a sheen to it that was like silk. It hugged his chest without being tight, showing off his well-developed muscles. A chef will have very good upper body muscles, I thought. A closer look told me his pants weren't jeans at all, but they fit like jeans. Again a beautiful fabric that clung without being tight. They showed me strong straight legs. *He will be quite beautiful without clothes.* A glance at his shoes—well, boots—showed again, expensive taste. They were leather, hand tooled, it appeared, with an intricate design on them.

A sigh of appreciation escaped my lips as I looked back up to his face.

"So I meet with your approval?" he asked with a smirk on his lips.

"Sorry, I didn't mean to do that, but you look very good tonight. I couldn't help but notice."

"I like to be appreciated, so thank you."

"You look good too. Very sexy," he said.

"I just threw a top and skirt over my swimsuit, figuring that was quickest. Glad you approve."

"My car is outside. Shall we?"

His car was parked in the back of the restaurant next door, which turned out to be a nice-looking steakhouse. *I must really get out of the hotel and try other restaurants!* Too bad I got "home" so late usually.

"You drive a Miata sports car?" I asked.

"Yes, just got her. Do you like it?"

"It's the car of my dreams to be honest. I have a Mazda myself, just not the Miata. And it's my color too: red."

"You want to drive?" he asked me.

"Can I for a while? You'll have to give me directions though."

"Of course," he said, throwing me the keys.

"AC or top down?" I asked.

"I always travel with the top down unless it is raining," he answered. He pressed the button to take the top off automatically.

"Now this is traveling in style!" I said.

Rick navigated me through the streets of Atlanta to the interstate. Once on the interstate it was pretty easy driving. It was a beautiful evening, and the sun was setting over our right shoulders as we headed south. I could swear the scent of the ocean became stronger the farther south we went. The open air of the car let us breathe in all the scents in the atmosphere.

"You can open her up if you want," Rick mentioned once we were on I-475.

"What do you call opened up?" I checked my speedometer, and I was already moving at seventy miles per hour.

"She is only taching 2500 right now, so she can handle a lot more," he answered.

"Okay," Watching the tachometer, I pushed her up to ninety and the dial barely hit 3500. What an engine. She was smooth too. It felt like we were flying. *What a feeling!* Surprisingly, the wind wasn't as bad as I had expected. My hair was up in a ponytail, so it didn't get tangled, but it was a good thing I brought a brush with me.

"So what would you like to listen to?" he asked. "Since I'm the passenger, the entertainment is my responsibility."

"Do you have Tom Cats?" I suggested.

"But of course!" He pulled out about six CDs and popped them all into the CD player in the car. "I had the sound system upgraded. It's a six CD player. It will automatically shuffle too."

The first song up was an old favorite, and we both started singing at the top of our lungs along with the music. It was great fun. We laughed at our off-key notes and settled into a camaraderie I hadn't expected. For a date, it was a good beginning.

We managed to get to Tallahassee in just under three hours, arriving at the door of the club by 8:30 p.m. I think we might have broken land-speed records for Miatas, but we hadn't been stopped by the police, so all was good. I was glad I got to drive.

Now for sure I'll be buying one of these for myself.

Rick took over and ushered me into the club and to a table at the front, on the edge of the dance floor.

"Rick, I need to order something to eat or I'm going to be drunk in no time," I said with a smirk.

"Okay, let me get the waiter." He motioned over a server to the table. "I'd like to order some food for our table please. What will you be drinking?" he asked me.

"I'd like a margarita please, classic, not crushed."

"I'll have the same," said Rick. "As well, bring a platter of wings and things."

"Very good, Mr. Benal. Right away," answered the waiter.

"Mr. Benal?" I asked.

"Yes, I'm a part owner in this club. It's how I knew the band was booked tonight."

"Oh really?" I asked. "You're full of surprises. So you're a sous-chef at the restaurant. What does a sous-chef do?" I asked.

"I'm the pastry chef," he replied, gauging my reaction.

"A pastry chef? That is interesting. Did you go to school to learn pastry arts, or did you learn on the job?"

"I went to school in Paris for my cooking degree. Then I spent a year in Germany learning Bavarian pastries, and a year in Switzerland learning confectionary skills."

"I'm impressed, so you're a real chef, not just a sous-chef! Very cool! What's your speciality?" I asked.

"Mille feuille," he said, but he said it like "mill fay."

I smiled at the American accent. You'd think living in Paris he'd have learned the correct pronunciation of the French term. But, to give him credit, there was no sound in English that sounded like *feuilles*.

"They're my favorite! J'adore mille feuilles!" I, of course, pronounced it right, so he didn't recognize the word.

"Huh? Oh yes, I just don't get how to make that sound. There is no equivalent in my native tongue," he laughed. "I got so used to calling them *mill fays* that I don't even notice anymore. Do you like the custard ones or the cream ones?"

"Oh, the best is a layer of each with the custard on the bottom, of course!" I answered.

He grinned. "You do know your mill fays. Okay, I thought you were spoofing me."

"I am from Montreal. Mille feuilles are standard fare at any good French-Canadian restaurant worth its salt. And in Montreal there are enough good restaurants to eat at a different one every day for a year!" I said proudly.

"I have heard of Montreal and always wanted to go there to study. There are some very good chefs there, and it's hard to get an understudy with them. Ironically, it was easier to get a placement in Paris."

"So how did you find the steakhouse to work at?" I asked.

"Actually, a fellow chef and I partnered up and we opened the restaurant about a year ago. My partner and I have been working very hard. It's a tough business.

"Your partner?"

"Just a business partner. He is the 'Chef Résidence,' and does all the menus except for the desserts and appetizers. We own the restaurant together. Our goal is to get big enough to open another."

"That is amazing. I will definitely have to come and eat there."

"Well, tell me when and I'll get you the best seat in the house," said Rick. "By the way, we're up for a culinary award this year too!"

"Oh, like a Michelin Star? Even I know that's a big deal. I hope you win!"

"You don't win a star, you need to earn it. Our restaurant is very new and not likely to earn a star yet, but we hope to. No, it's a James Beard Award."

"So, do you cook?" he asked.

"Yes, but I'm not a pastry chef. My mom is a very good cook and I have learned well from her. She was talented enough that she got into the Cordon Bleu school in Paris but couldn't go because it was wartime. A missed opportunity, sadly. But I do make a good pie pastry—the old-fashioned way."

"Hmmm, we'll have to have a bake-off then. Your pie against my *mill fay*!" he challenged me.

"Hey, I don't think that will be a fair fight! How about pie against pie?" I suggested.

"Okay, you're on. You can come by the restaurant and we can bake up some pies together," he offered.

"Wow, to use a commercial kitchen? That would be a dream! Sure, count me in. Would we be allowed though?" I asked.

"If the restaurant is closed, yes. Oh, but you work during the day, don't you?"

"Yes, I do. Don't you?"

"No, most of my hours are at night. We don't make the food too far in advance so that it is fresh. So things like the whipped cream have to be made on the spot. I usually start at three o'clock and work until 2:00 a.m."

"Oh, that's why this trip at this hour is not daunting to you! You're used to being up this late all the time," I said.

"Yes, but don't worry. You can curl up in the car and sleep on the way home if you like."

I tried to picture myself doing that in the Miata. There wasn't a lot of room for "curling up," and with the top down it was pretty noisy and windy.

"I don't think I'll be sleeping in the car, but you never know."

"I keep the top up at night because of bugs," he said. "As for curling up, you can put your head on my lap as a pillow."

I was thinking about that when the lights dimmed and the announcement that the band was about to come on was made.

Bobby peeked through the curtain at the back and noticed me in the front row of tables and immediately came over to say hello.

"What a pleasant surprise, sunshine. Thank you for coming down, Falon!" said Bobby, hugging me quickly. He looked at Rick and shook his hand. "Enjoy the show, folks." Then he retreated behind the curtain.

Rick looked at me with some respect when that happened. He might have some star value in his job, but Bobby Styles knew me by name. How cool was that?

The Tom Cats burst out from the back of the stage to loud cheering and a standing ovation. When the clapping and cheering settled down, everyone took their seats.

"Thank you everyone for the warm welcome! We are Bobby Styles and the Tom Cats!" said Bobby into the mic.

The music started, and right away people were up on the floor dancing, including us. It was nice to have someone to dance with, and Rick was doing pretty good too. I'd completely forgotten that I was still wearing my bathing suit under my shirt and skirt, but remembered when I was getting really hot dancing. When I returned to the table to leave my shirt, people were giving me strange looks.

"Wow, that may be too sexy for this place," said Rick, "but I like it."

"It's just the shock of me taking off my blouse, I guess. We do it all the time in Montreal. Us girls are always taking our blouses off when we get hot dancing."

Rick was studying me closely while we danced. Finally, he smiled and said, "You're teasing me, right?"

"Only a little," I said, laughing. "Actually, layering is how I handle getting overheated."

Of course, the advantage of wearing a one-piece swimsuit for dancing was that it acted like a bodysuit. Only thin straps criss-crossed my back, and the seat of the suit was below the skirt waistline, so it looked like my entire back was naked. The neckline of the suit was fairly low, but there was structure to the suit so it both perked up my breasts and held them down by compression. At least I wasn't bouncing around too much. My only potential problem was the zipper. I had to make sure it didn't unzip without me knowing or other people noticing it too much.

The music slowed down for a couple of songs as the Tom Cats sang some ballads. Rick immediately closed the gap between us, holding me closely against him. As we started swaying and moving to the first ballad, he took in me in a waltz-like position and I rested my free hand on his upper arm. He had firm muscles in his arm.

"Mmmm, you've got nice muscles," I remarked to him.

"It must be all the mixing I do," he mused. He pressed his athletic body against me while we were hot and sweaty. The motion was erotic, especially since I could feel him coming up against me.

One hand was down at the small of my back, the other gently pressed my head against his chest. It's nice to be with a guy that is tall enough that you fit under his arm and your head can rest on the soft part of his chest. Another bonus, the fabric of his shirt was not damp. Those muscles I saw earlier under his beautifully fit shirt were well-defined under my cheek. He had a pleasant, musky scent too, from the sweat of dancing.

We danced that way for three songs, then the Tom Cats called a break. Regretfully, we broke the hold of the dance and walked back to our table and took our seats. Rick and I sat in a comfortable silence for a few minutes while I downed a glass of water.

Motioning to the waiter, Rick ordered more drinks immediately.

Bobby stopped by again. "So, Falon, I'm so glad to see you again. Twice in one weekend. You're setting up to be a super fan!"

"This was a surprise," I answered Bobby. "Rick here invited me, and it was an offer I couldn't refuse," I said with a big smile.

"Well, I'll let you two enjoy yourselves. Thanks again for coming," said Bobby. He went backstage again, but not before I got a promise out of him for my two favorite songs.

I excused myself to go to the ladies' room. Winding my way through the crowd, I was getting lots of looks, so I glanced down at myself and discovered I had spilled water over my chest and the zipper was undone to the middle of my chest. My breasts were almost popping out. Huh, cleavage! I casually raised the zipper, but not all the way to the top. Hey, I never got this kind of attention at home. I was going to enjoy it a bit.

When I returned to the table, Rick apparently had the same call, because he wasn't there. I took my seat again and sipped on the fresh margarita that had arrived. They were delicious, tart and strong, and even though I had been dancing, I was starting to feel the tequila working on me. I would have to slow down the alcohol consumption, or dance more!

I was humming and tapping my foot on the floor to a replaying of one of the songs in my head when a guy sat down beside me and suggestively put his arm around the back of my chair, and leaned close to my ear.

"Hey, little lady, wanna have a real Southern gentleman?" he whispered, looking at my chest lewdly.

"No, thanks, I have a date," I answered him.

"Ah, that one can't satisfy the likes of you," he said. "He's too skinny and thin. You need a real brawny Southern man," he said huskily.

"I suppose that means you?" I asked, turning around to look at him. It was that Derek character again. "What the hell are you doing here? Are you following me?"

"No, but it looks like we're being drawn together. Don't you feel it?" he rasped. "I can set you on fire with my dick."

"No, I don't feel anything toward you," I assured him. "You won't be lighting me with anything."

"Com'on now, don't play hard to get. Come sit on my lap and see," he said as he reached for my thigh with his free hand he wrapped his other arm around my waist and dragged me off my chair onto his lap. That left hand had migrated up under my skirt and was making its way between my legs.

Struggling against him only caused him to grin widely as he had clamped his arm strongly around me. I only succeeded in elbowing him in the ribs, which hurt me as much as it hurt him, but he didn't let go. Hopefully the one piece swimsuit would stop him. His stinky breath was hot on my neck as I continued to struggle against his arm.

"Take your hands off me, you pervert!" I yelled as loudly as I could. That at least brought attention to the fact that he was molesting me.

"Ah shucks," he said. "She's just a little wired right now folks. Never mind."

The people who had turned around, went back to their conversations leaving him with this jerk.

By the second time I was going to yell at him Rick was there to come to my rescue. Pulling the guy's arm away from my body, he lifted me off the guy's lap and held me close as I gained my feet under me. He placed himself between me and the guy. Very gallant, but I didn't think it would be a good idea. That guy was strong!

The jerk jumped up, dumping his chair onto the floor and towering over Rick menacingly. To Rick's credit, he didn't cower or flinch one iota. He seemed to get taller, as he pushed me behind him and shielded me with his own body.

"The lady said no," he said quietly.

"I don't care what the bitch said, she's askin' for it!" yelled Derek.

"Back off, or security will remove you," Rick said. You had to strain to hear him over the din of the crowd.

"Hand her over, dick, she's my hottie for the night," Derek sneered.

"Security!" Rick called. And then there were four beefy black guys standing all around us.

"Do you need help, Mr. Benal?" one of the bouncers asked.

"Could you please remove this hoodlum from our facility?" Rick asked politely.

"Certainly, Mr. Benal. Right away." The two bouncers grabbed the jerk by both of his arms. They picked him up off the floor so his feet were kicking as they carried him out of the bar.

"Right this way, sir." They guided him through the tables and escorted him to the door. After he was removed from the table, Rick turned to me with a worried look on his face.

"Are you alright? Did that scum hurt you?" he asked, concerned.

"No, I'm fine. Just a little embarrassed, I guess."

"Why? What have you done to be embarrassed? He assaulted you!" Rick was angry. "We try to make sure these jerks don't get the upper hand, but you never know who's going to become a jerk until they do."

I was starting to react to the assault. My brain functions were slowing down, I could tell. That creep had got further than he should have. Normally, I can deal with these assholes without a problem. But this one, he got to me. Perhaps it was because I wasn't on home territory? Being away in a strange place? I don't know. But it shook me up when it hadn't before.

"Yes. Would you like to leave?" he asked. "I would completely understand after what has happened here."

"No, no, no, I don't want to leave. We'll miss the Tom Cats! I just need to dance, and drink."

Another margarita appeared in front of me. My other glass was gone, but it had been down to the ice. I glanced around, and even though I felt as though a spotlight had been put on me, I was relieved to see that no one was looking our way. It was as though I was not even there, and what had happened had not. I felt myself relax a little. Perhaps I could enjoy more of this great night after all. I took a sip of the drink. Ah ha! They had made this one stronger—I could really taste the tequila.

The Tom Cats were back and soon everyone was happy and jiving again. When they played the *Tom Cat Crawl,* I got a dedication. How nice! I was singing along with the music and dancing along to the lyrics. Bobby hopped down off the stage with me and we strode across the floor in time to the music. What fun!

A second break, and then a third set, and the night was over. The house lights were coming up and people were getting up to leave. I was sad because I didn't want this night to end. Rick stuck by my side all night, being the perfect partner and a great date.

The margaritas kept coming all night and I was a little high by the end. Rick had to help me walk to the car. His arm was around my waist and we "crawled" to the car, singing out loud. He slipped me into the passenger side, swinging my legs in and closing the door.

He got into the driver's side and put the key in the ignition. He turned toward me on the seat and quietly asked, "How about we get a room here in Tallahassee?"

I was bagged and a lot drunk! One should never go to a hotel when one is drunk. You don't have control of your decisions. Oh, but I wanted to.

"Wait, can you even drive?" I asked.

"Yes, I've been drinking plain sparkling water all night. I expected to drive."

"Oh wow, what a sacrifice. Thank you. I may be a little too drunk to make good decisions right now. I think we'd better get back tonight if you can drive."

"It wasn't a sacrifice. I think I can drive fine. So if you would prefer going back, I completely understand," he said.

"Crap! Why do you have to be such a gentleman?" I said under my breath.

"Pardon me?"

Ooops, did I say that out loud?

"Well, if for any reason you feel you can't drive anymore, pull off and we'll sleep, okay?"

"Yes, ma'am. For now, make yourself comfortable."

I did. I managed to find a way to bend over and put my head on his lap as he suggested. He stroked my hair as he drove. I was acutely aware of what I was lying on too. Every now and then I felt a little twitch.

I could very easily unzip these pants and play with his toys. I think I want to.

Sometime later, Rick was gently shaking my shoulder.

"Wake up, Falon. I have to stop driving. I'm sorry, but my eyes are crossing. There is a motel just off the highway here, so I'm going to stop there."

"Mmmm, that's fine. I'm comfy right here. You do what you want." My hand was on his bulge, and I was caressing it lightly. It seemed like the thing to do.

I fell asleep again twisted in my seat with my fingers touching him. When the car stopped moving, I woke up, startled. Sitting up, I looked around and saw him walking back to the car.

It looked like a clean motel.

"I've got two rooms for us," he said as he opened the door.

"Two rooms?"

"Were you expecting something different?" he asked. There was a slight smirk on his lips. He was being that gentleman again. "They are adjoining rooms, so we can open up the door between them if you like."

We each went into our room, and I tried to lie down. Being restless, I went and knocked on the adjoining door. Rick opened it with a big grin on his face.

"Can't sleep?" he asked me.

"Nah, actually I was just going to say thank you for everything tonight. You've been an absolute gentleman and I've really enjoyed myself and had a great night. It's been one of the best dates I've ever had."

"Even with the jerk?"

"Especially because of the jerk. I've never had a guy jump to my defense like that before!" I blushed a bit.

I walked through the door and he took me in his arms. He held me carefully, tightly but not squeezing. I could feel his breath on the top of my head.

"I'm very glad you had a good time. I was very happy you called and that I could bring you with me. It wouldn't have been nearly as much fun without you," he said. And for the first time I could hear emotion in his voice.

"May I kiss you goodnight?" he asked.

"Do all Southern gentlemen ask before they do something?" I wondered out loud, thinking back to another experience.

"They do if they are gentlemen," he answered simply.

"Yes, I would like that," I answered him. And with that he reached down and kissed me lightly at first, then more deeply. I could feel the tequila stupor lifting and my body awakening. When he broke the kiss, I felt a little weak in the knees. A good kiss has that effect.

I kissed him back, and the kiss became hungry and demanding. Our bodies squeezed together with a ripe energy. He broke the kiss again. My knees were definitely weak this time as I almost slumped down. He caught me, picked me up and took me to my bed.

"Good night and sleep tight. I'll keep the doors open in case you need me," he said.

Then he let me go and walked back to his room. It was only then, by the light coming through the windows, I saw that he wasn't wearing a shirt. I was still in my bathing suit. I got up and removed my shirt and skirt and unzipped my suit. Then I walked back into his room to stand and look at him, with the moon shining on his body. Every curve was outlined in shadow from the perfectly formed pectorals to the six-pack of his abdomen.

I walked to the edge of the bed and knelt down to kiss him goodnight. My suit was completely unzipped, so when I leaned over, my breasts hung down.

His eyes opened and caught me leaning over him. He took hold of me and pulled me down on top of me. I leaned over and kissed him hungrily. Sitting up, I undid his pants and let his shaft come out to play. He reached up and flipped me over and held me down with his body weight.

The next kiss wasn't so gentle; his mouth demanded my surrender. I did … surrender. As his hands expertly cupped my breast and caressed it, he forsook my mouth to kiss and suck on my breast.

Fires started to spread up from my core as his sucking became nips and licks. I was getting so aroused I needed to not just lie there.

My hand found him and I started to caress his shaft. The velvety softness was hot to touch, and it danced in my hand as I rubbed him.

"Ahh, Falon, I would love to make love to you right now. My body has been responding to you all night."

"Me too, Rick. Undress me. Please."

And so he pulled off the suit. As it was freed from my hips, he was kneeling between my legs. He didn't need to pry them apart as he leaned down to kiss my mound. His breath sent tingles all over my skin. He delicately opened my flower with his fingers and took my clit in his lips.

"Ahhh!" I gasped. "Oh yes! More please," I cried.

He sucked on my clit like he did on my breast, alternating between that and licking me.

"Your nectar is so sweet," he murmured. "It's like honey to me." He took a long slow lick of my entire slit. As he passed over my vagina, he dipped his tongue inside a moment.

I growled.

His fingers took over my clit as his tongue pierced my vagina. He pushed in as far as he could, which was pretty far, and brought me nearly to a climax. Changing to fingers, he inserted two and started finger-fucking me. Reaching the g-spot just inside the opening was key to maximum stimulation.

Working both g-spots at once built up the wave in me faster than ever. I was jerking, and my hips were moving in rhythm to his fingers before I knew it.

With a great explosive release, I climaxed as he was applying tongue and fingers.

"Oh my God, Rick … oh my God … oh my God, Rick please, ahhhhh," I screamed out.

A few minutes later, Rick lay beside me covering my nakedness with his. A tender kiss accompanied his presence, as I drifted off to sleep contented from the wonderful climax he had given me. I had interesting dreams that night.

10— Here Comes the Rain Again

When I woke up the next morning, it was still dark. There was a disorienting pounding on the wall.

I looked around, confused as to where I was. Then I remembered. Rick had pleasured me last night expertly, and I had fallen asleep on him. Oh my! How embarrassing. I wanted to have sex with him. All the indications were it would be wonderful.

The pounding continued.

I stood up, and that was a mistake. Oh now it was pounding behind my eyes.

Tequila! Oh ya, I overindulged last night. A flash of light split my vision, leaving stars floating in the air. Then another crash. A thunderstorm was happening. Okay, that wasn't helping!

I turned to look at the clock beside the bed and my head felt like it was in a vise. *I am going to pay for this all day.* The face on the clock told me it was 5:15 a.m. That was a good thing; it would give me a chance to have a shower and get dressed before we had to leave.

I was still in Rick's bed and he was nowhere to be seen. I got out of bed, saw I was naked, smiled at the memory, and went in search of my swimsuit, which I found on the back of a chair. Yuck, it smelled of tequila, smoke, and sweat. Perhaps I could wash it while I was in the shower before putting it back on.

Walking around the bed, I took a moment to glance into my room. Rick was not in that bed either. He must have been woken up by the storm too. Maybe he was in the shower. I walked into the bathroom; the door was open but he was not in there. Wondering where he could be, I walked to the window to see if I could see his Miata, but we didn't park close to our rooms. So I went for my shower.

As I was standing under the hot water, fighting the urge to vomit, I thought about what I would do if he didn't come back. I'd find a way into Atlanta on my own. *There's got to be a bus somewhere. Oh God, I need aspirin, shampoo, and soap, in that order.* Getting out of the shower, I found and swallowed the aspirin first, then grabbing the shampoo I jumped back under the water. I shampooed my hair to thoroughly wash last night's stink out of it. Next me, my vagina with soap. I tingled as I washed myself. I fantasized about his fingers, and that got me all aroused again.

At least half an hour later I finally felt human again and was ready to get out of the shower. I pulled the curtain open as I wiped the water from my eyes with my other hand. When I opened my eyes, Rick was standing in the doorway dressed, with two coffees in his hand, watching me.

"Good morning! Enjoying the show?" I said as I grabbed a towel.

"Very much. You look very sexy all wet. I just want to lick you dry now. May I?" he said with a smile.

"Is that coffee I smell?" I asked.

"Yes, I hadn't expected you to be awake yet, and I was bringing you breakfast in bed. Alas, it was impossible to find crescents," Rick explained.

"Crescents? Oh, croissants! Gotcha! That was very nice of you, especially in this rain. But I need to get dressed."

"I'll set up breakfast in the other room." He walked back to his room, but he didn't close the doors. I dressed quickly. At least my swimsuit was freshened, if damp, and the skirt would cover that. I didn't need to put the blouse back on.

We ate breakfast fast and checked out.

"Do you think we'll get back to Atlanta before 8:30?" I asked Rick once we were back on the road.

"I think so," he said. "I need to pick up some clothes at my place, but then we'll go straight to the hotel. I estimate we should be there by 8:30ish."

"That is going to be close for me. I need to be at work by 9:00, and it's a half an hour drive. Would you mind driving me straight to the hotel please?"

"Okay, if you think you need to, yes."

Wait a minute! It was Sunday, I don't need to go to work.

"Never mind—I forgot it was Sunday. We can go to your place on the way as you suggested." I said, changing my mind.

"Okay, thanks," said Rick. "How do you feel this morning?"

"About what? The drinking, the dancing, the wonderful oral sex?" I asked.

"Yes," he chuckled.

"I had a perfect time last night. Thank you for taking me to Tallahassee. As far as the oral sex is concerned, wow! I'm so sorry I fell asleep on you. That's not fair! I owe you now."

"You owe me nothing. I loved giving you pleasure. Your body responds deliciously."

"Only when it's played right," I said, remembering what the sex was like with Brandon.

"I can't imagine not playing it right," he answered. "You mean to tell me some men do not pleasure the woman first?"

"Not all. My ex-husband hated sex, so it was an in and out affair, literally. Wham, bam, thank you, ma'am—not. Some men take their time, they're the best—the ones who explore. Others can't keep it in their pants long enough. That's sad."

"I can keep it in my pants," he said as a challenge.

"I noticed, and it was a nice package too. I'm disappointed in myself that I didn't get to open it up."

"We'll do something about that," he assured me.

We sat in silence for a while, each of us thinking our own thoughts. I watched his face out of the corner of my eye.

"You know, I've never fallen asleep on a man before," I started.

"Neither have I," he smirked. "Fallen asleep, I mean." Then he laughed. "Sorry, this is me on no sleep."

"Didn't you sleep last night?" I asked him.

"No, not much. I couldn't get to sleep because I was spending the night with a beautiful woman naked next to me. I almost woke you up three or four times, but figured you needed your rest. So I spent most of the night watching you sleep. You've got a cute little smile when you sleep, when you're not snoring."

"I snore?"

"A little. In bursts and spurts. Not a deep train sound."

"Wait, you watched me sleep all night? That is odd, Rick," I said.

"Well, I just wanted to hold you. You were curled up in my arms when I pulled the sheet up to keep us warm. You snuggled into me, and I had a very contented feeling just being there. I really had a wonderful time last night. I want to spend more time with you if you feel the same."

"I do ... feel the same way," I said. "I am sorry I fell asleep on you."

"Okay, no more apologies. From either of us. Deal?"

"Deal."

We fell silent again. I was watching the countryside go by. It was a completely different type of landscape compared to home. Different trees, different birds, even the rain was different. It was coming down hard and beating against the windshield. I focused forward. I knew just how difficult the driving probably was. You could hardly see past the end of the hood. The road was disappearing in front of us as we went. I let Rick concentrate on the driving and didn't distract him.

The rain started to let up by the time we passed Macon. We were almost back to Atlanta now, about another hour. Rick was relaxing his grip on the steering wheel a bit and his shoulders were not as hunched from the strain of driving.

"You want to put on some music? I can handle it now that I don't have to focus so much on the road."

"Sure thing."

I was flipping through the dial when I felt his hand caress my back as I bent over. It lightly went up and down my back, resting on my waist. His fingertips sent shivers down my spine. When I found a good, strong radio station, I sat back in my seat. His hand came forward and rested on my leg near the junction of leg and body. So I placed my hand on his leg, close to his crotch to feel his heat as well.

It was almost 8:00 and we were coming up the 75 and were almost back to Sandy Springs. We turned off the highway onto a local road and the scenery changed into an affluent neighborhood. Neatly groomed houses on large lots—at least large by my standards—lined the wide streets. Big trees along one side of the street indicated that it was a well-established neighborhood. Rick turned into a driveway that was red stone. The house was large and modern. Huge glass windows were taking up almost the entire first floor on the front of the house. There was a palm tree in the garden, a huge one.

"Palm trees, nice. I'd love to have a palm tree, but of course they don't live in our climate. Palm trees always mean vacation to me—it would be like living in a vacation spot all the time."

"Come on in," invited Rick.

"Sure." I followed him. I was having trouble believing this wasn't his parents' house or something. Were chefs that successful? There was beautiful ceramic tile from the entryway all the way through the first floor. It was an open concept house; all the rooms were floating in their own space without walls to anchor them.

"There should be coffee in the kitchen, right through that way," he pointed. "I have it programmed to make coffee automatically every day."

"Waking up to good coffee all the time must be nice. I have that at home, but not in the hotel. The machines they put in the rooms are not really good."

"I'll be just a minute," he said as he ran up the stairs. I heard the shower go on and a door close, so I decided to be nosy this time. I went into the kitchen—which was stunning—and found the coffee maker and some cups. I poured two cups and carried them upstairs in the direction Rick had gone. I found his room, and it was indeed the master bedroom. The ensuite bathroom was amazing. It had a huge Jacuzzi tub in the middle with a large glass-enclosed shower off to one side. The shower had what looked like ten nozzles of water. I stood there spying on him a little. I could see his shape through the water, a perfect Y shape with great obliques. He had a nice ass too. I thought he would after seeing him in his pants. That's all I could see for now.

I placed his coffee on the counter by the sink and leaned against the door jam, watching him. Slim, yes, but muscular. I had felt the strength in those arms last night when we were dancing and when he picked me up off that jerk. I had also felt the muscles in his abdomen and chest. This man worked on his body and kept fit. I guess that was important if you were a pastry chef. Imagine how easy it would be to get fat when you were making pastries and desserts all day long…

Big blobs of bubbles were sluicing down his back, following the path of the water down off his shoulder to the small of his back, and then down between his buns. I wanted to jump in with him. I was about to put my coffee down and strip and get in with him, when he turned around and saw me.

He laughed. "Ah ha! Like what you see?"

"Um, yeah, it's a very pleasant view. You've a nice body, too. Worth admiring. Very much worth admiring," I admitted. "I'll tell you what, turn around and I'll wash your back for you."

"Okay. But you'll get wet," he said.

"Yes, but I'm wearing a swimsuit, remember? It doesn't matter if it gets wet."

"Oh, yeah." He looked a little disappointed as he turned around. I jumped out of my skirt and unzipped my swimsuit. I decided I would keep it on and see where it would go from there. Of course, the fact that this was going to make me late for work didn't seem to enter into my brain at that moment. The only thing I could think about was the wet body in front of me.

Opening the door, I stepped into the shower behind him. The water was almost scalding.

"Yikes!"

"Oh, is it too hot for you?" he asked.

"Give me a minute, I'll adjust."

He handed me a sponge with soap in it and stepped forward a little.

I started soaping his back in circles at his shoulders. He was taller than me, just the way I liked it, so I had to reach a bit. Working my way down his back, I kept making the circles until I got to his buttocks. I could feel him tense ever so slightly as I touched his butt. I kept the sponge moving all over him and then I got to the top of his legs. He had been standing with his legs apart. Now I could see him from the back. He was saluting!

I changed the motion of my hand from circular to up and down along the length of his legs. When I reached between his legs with the sponge to wash him, he almost jumped out of the shower. He looked down at me over his shoulder. I was kneeling on the floor, my swimsuit was completely open, and I was wet.

Rick turned around then and I came face to face with his erection. That made him blush! He reached down and lifted me off my knees to my feet. Then he kissed me again with a passion that told of promise. One hand was behind my back, pulling me into him, and the other was working its way into my swimsuit to cup my breast. Meanwhile, not to be outdone, his erection was pushing inside my suit at the base of the zipper.

The kiss was long and soft as his tongue caressed mine. When we pulled apart, I was winded. He had a dreamy look on his face. He looked down at himself and was about to apologize, when I placed my finger on his lips to quiet him.

I shushed him. "Don't apologize for arousal. It's a compliment. If you hadn't been, I would have worried that there was something wrong with me."

"You have aroused me several times since the first time I met you." He looked embarrassed. "The first time was when you called me on the bag line. You were so sexy to me that I knew I had to make a fool of myself and try to get a date with you." He laughed. "Last night dancing, oh my God, I couldn't believe you were with me! I had the sexiest, most beautiful woman in the place. I was so proud. It absolutely made my heart soar to know you. It was quite the coup for me because everyone thinks I'm not interested in women. It's only because I've never found a woman who has interested me."

"I find it hard to imagine you being gay, but then I've got to know you."

"I couldn't believe it when you knew Bobby Styles either. That was way too cool."

"Yeah, I met him at the hotel, coincidentally the day before. So it felt cool to be known."

"When I got back to the table and that jerk was mauling you, I almost crushed him. If I hadn't left, you wouldn't have been put in that situation. I felt so bad. But you were so brave."

"I've had some experience with jerks. He was strong though, so I really appreciated the save this time. This particular one has been harassing me for a couple of days."

"Really? Was he at the hotel too?"

"That's where I saw him first, by the pool. Hopefully he's gone now."

"I just want to say, last night, giving you pleasure, watching you respond to my touch, that was exciting and made me want you even more. This morning, watching you get out of the shower, I barely contained myself and stopped from taking you right there and then. I knew I wanted you more than anything else in my life. I had to take a moment to set breakfast out, or the hard-on I had right then almost made me lose it.

"When we were discussing our trip home in the car, I half-wanted you to ask me to drop you off first because I wanted to get you home here and just be with you. After you agreed to come here first, I was soaring, but I was so tense because I knew I would need to control myself. Now here you are wet and nearly naked in my shower. I'm so hard right now, I'm not going to be able to get dressed." He grinned broadly. "What am I going to do with you?"

"My, that was quite the speech! I have a few ideas," I answered flirtatiously, and I grasped him in my hands. I could feel him quiver under my touch. But he pulled away from me and put my hands back at my sides. I pouted.

"Not yet," he said.

Then he caressed my breast one more time and zipped up my suit, opened the door to the shower, and led me out. He didn't bother wrapping a towel around either. Instead he stood us under some contraption on the ceiling and several seconds later a strong downdraft of warm air started drying us off.

"Now that is a neat device!" I said.

"It's pretty good for taking the worst of the water off the body. They use these in Europe instead of towels. I liked it so much, I had a large blower installed in the house."

He led us directly into the bedroom where he unzipped my swimsuit again and slowly peeled it off. As the suit got lower, he kissed his way down my body. He let the suit drop around my ankles and stood up and took me into his arms again. We were there interlocked by a kiss and an embrace. I could feel him getting more aroused.

He picked me up and carried me to the bed and knelt on the edge. He started kissing me some more, on my breasts, shoulders, the inside of my elbows, under my breasts, down my tummy, right down to my hairline as he slid to the floor. I was becoming very aroused. He spread my legs and lifted them up so my whole slit was exposed to him. He took his time sucking on my clit and licking up my wetness.

He stood up and I wrapped my legs around his hips and held on to him as he deftly opened me up with his fingertips. He guided his head to my doorway, and I could feel the small spasms of excitement next to my skin.

He was teasing me as he rubbed himself up and down my slit, getting himself wet on my juices. As he gently pushed inside I could feel his excitement go through him. Once his head was inside, he paused to feel us connected, and to give me a minute, I guess.

"You fill me nicely," I complimented him.

"Thank you, I'm not too much for you?" he asked.

"Not at all."

"That's been a complaint before. It's why I've not been with a lot of women."

"You feel good to me. No need to be cautious," I reassured him.

His cock waggled in response to me squeezing him and I felt him expand as he let himself go. He stopped and looked into my eyes questioningly.

"Please," was all I could say.

The phone rang just as he pushed himself fully inside. He paused for a moment, listening.

The answering machine got it. He was about to continue when he recognized the voice on the phone and stopped.

"Rick, Justin here. I hope you're home, buddy, from your jaunt down to Tallahassee. Miranda Cook is here and she is bloody mad that you're not. Apparently, you had an interview booked with her for a review she was doing for the *Michelin Guide*. So if you're there, you bloody well get your ass here now! And I mean on the double! I don't care what you're doing, or *who* for that matter!"

"Crap! Fuck! Damn it all to hell!" Rick swore and then stood up, looked at me longingly, and then pulled out carefully. He was fully engorged.

"I am really sorry. I've got to go. I forgot completely about this, and if I piss this woman off, she'll sink my restaurant. "How am I ever going to get dressed with this?" he asked me with a grin, gesturing to his erection. He returned to the shower for two seconds, came back wet again, and went to the light switches next to the door.

While the air dried his body, his erection shriveled. Rick walked over to me and took me in his arms tenderly again. Then he pulled back and looked me in the face. "Falon, dear, I would like nothing more than to make love to you right now and keep you here all day long in bed with me, but I have to run. Please say we will get together again, no? Surely you won't ditch me after one date?"

"No, Rick, I won't ditch you after one date."

I was trying to get my own emotions back under control too. We got dressed again quickly, and he dropped me off at the front door of the hotel. When I walked into the hotel dressed the same way I went out last night, Franco at the front desk looked at me and winked.

Brother, I was going to have a big reputation here soon. I'd have to change hotels! I was very lucky today was Sunday. I could just relax today. I ran upstairs, got changed into clean clothes, and sat there trying to figure out what to do today.

I know what I wanted to do—that was to finish what got interrupted! But that would depend on Rick's availability. Until then, perhaps some breakfast, because it was Sunday brunch, and a swim.

I ran into Ray in the lobby, strangely. He took one look at me and smiled.

"What are you doing here?" I asked.

"I was here with someone last night."

"But why this hotel?"

"The company puts up all our guests in this hotel. We have a corporate rate."

"So you bring your dates here?"

"Why not?" he said with a grin. "I sure hope he was good! 'Cause you look like it was an all-nighter!" He walked away chuckling.

I went for brunch.

11—Reflections

Between the night with Brandon in the hot tub, the trip to Tallahassee with Rick, and seeing the Tom Cats twice, this weekend was a wild ride. I was tired to say the least. It was amazingly fun, but strangely unsatisfying.

I found Ray at another table in the restaurant with a pot of coffee and a spread of books in front of him.

"This is becoming a habit of yours—meeting people here?" I asked.

"I was meeting another potential client. That gentleman from Germany I was telling you about."

"Oh. That is not the one I have to go to dinner with, is it?"

"No, not the same. He's in town tomorrow. So find something pretty and feminine to wear, okay?"

Caroline walked into the restaurant and sat beside Ray. Her face had a strange expression on it. She looked at Ray and got up and left abruptly.

"I'll be waiting," she said, and walked toward the elevators.

"Ray, you know you should really not do that. It is not good for the morale of the other girls," I chastised him.

"I'll get to them sooner or later," he countered. "All in good time."

"See you later, Ray," I said, rolling my eyes at him.

"Wait, I have a gift for you," he said. He reached into his briefcase and pulled out a box.

I opened the box to discover it was a new copy of Microsoft Project.

"Thanks, this piece of software will change my life," I said. "I'll get on it right away."

Tomorrow is soon enough. Today was Sunday. I went back to my room, sat down, and my body felt pretty tired.

Pretty and feminine? Did he think he was pimping me out or something?

I lay down on the bed and crashed. I ended up sleeping until almost dinner. Waking up, I felt refreshed, and decided to have a long soak in the tub. Once in the luxurious hot water, my mind started to reflect on the events of the past weekend.

It was exciting to go on the road trip with Rick, spontaneous. I'd rarely done anything on the spur of the moment, and it had felt good. I had to be more like that, to grab the opportunities that dropped in my lap. I wished we had been able to finish what we started. Talk about coitus interruptus.

I had way too much tequila though. *Note to self—easy on the tequila*. Dancing was nice. *Wow, he's the owner of the bar and the restaurant*. That was a surprise.

I almost felt bad about driving back last night. Stopping at the motel was the smart thing to do, and as it turned out he was a great lover, at least what I'd seen so far. He certainly knew his way around a woman's body.

There were apparently lots of good-looking men in Atlanta. God knows, I kept being approached by them. But good looking is not the be all and end all. I still believed it was because I looked so different from the women down here. Being Irish Canadian, I was darker, and I was tanned from the sun. Most of the Southern women I had met so far were fair and pale-skinned because they avoided the sun—well, avoided the heat.

Dare I judge these guys on a rating system? I was not looking at any of them as boyfriend material; they all lived away from me. *So okay, let's put them on a scale.*

Looks: Mark was a Greek god, chiseled olive skin, dark curly hair, perfect body. *He's a ten.*

Brandon was a fair-haired Southern boy. Fair-skinned, light blue eyes, fine features, slim build but strong. *I'd say he's a nine.*

Rick was a Latin lover, darked eyed, brown skinned, thick black hair, slim, wiry, strong, and well muscled. His Latin features gave him a steam setting of twelve. *So he's also a ten.*

Intellectually: I thought Rick somehow edged Mark out on this one. Maybe because he was a pastry chef. Mark was wise like anything. Brandon was a musician. Not intellectual at all.

Sexually: I'd only got two out of three who finished in that respect, and of those two there was a clear and undeniable winner: Mark. *Rick may be a serious contender though.*

I still needed a larger sample to judge from.

Fun: Rick got top marks for that too. Brandon was a close second, and Mark so far was in third place.

Emotionally: there was much more depth in both Rick and Mark than Brandon. That was a matter of age and knowing what they wanted. Both of those men knew what they wanted and how to get it. *Is there capacity to love me and me love them?* Yes, I could fall for Rick. I'd already fallen for Mark. No, I couldn't fall for Brandon.

Now … there was another ingredient I hadn't taken into consideration: supernatural. There was no doubt that Zisis made life very interesting. Mark had done nothing like that … yet. Of course neither Rick nor Brandon could compete on that one at all.

Was there a clear winner? I needed a larger sample for sure. I grinned to myself. Life was so hard sometimes! I needed to call Lora tonight. *I wish I could get her down here! We'd have so much fun!*

I soaked in the tub until the water was cooling off. When I got out, I was all wrinkled like a prune. Time to order room service.

Franco answered the front desk.

"Ms. Robertson, how can I help you?"

"I'd like to order room service please."

"Go ahead."

"May I please have a grilled cheese sandwich on white bread, a bowl of tomato soup, and a glass of skim milk? Is that possible?"

"Not impossible at all. Would you like anything else with that?" he asked.

"Mmmm, how about some dessert? What do you have today?" I asked.

"The restaurant next door delivered some mille feuilles this afternoon for us. They appear to be very good. Would you like one of those?"

"That would be nice," I agreed. He even pronounced the name correctly!

"It will be about fifteen minutes, Ms. Robertson."

"Thank you, Franco."

"I have two messages for you today," he said.

"You can give them to me now."

"Mr. Ricardo Benal called first, and he called twice. Mr. Brandon of the band left the message 'Will you be in tonight?'"

"I do not have Mr. Benal's number."

I didn't want to talk to men tonight. I wanted a quiet night, possibly a book with my room service. And I wanted to call Lora.

I was just about to call Lora when there was a knock on the door.

"Room service!"

"Just a moment please." I looked out the peephole and saw the tray waiting for me.

I opened the door and the man rolled the tray into the room. I gave him a tip, and he left.

Now I could call Lora.

"Hello," answered Lora.

"Hi, it's me."

"Oh good, I was wondering how you were doing."

"Well, this past weekend was a wild ride."

"Do tell!"

I recited a play-by-play of my evening at the bar with the band and how I had made friends with the keyboardist and ended up in a hot tub on the roof.

"Friday night the house band played. They were really good! I danced and the band came and sat with me. I also met some of the staff and they joined the party. It was a good night."

"Sounds like a fun night."

"It didn't end there."

"What else?"

"The leader of the house band, Brandon, and I got busy in the hot tub on the roof."

"You what?"

"What I said. It was hot—in the hot tub." I giggled at my own joke. "I had sex with Brandon in a hot tub that same night."

"So, how was it?"

"Meh. On a scale of one to ten, about a six."

"Ouch. Why so low?"

"Well, it was fun, but it was just a shag. You know what I mean. Guy gets off but doesn't really care whether the woman is satisfied. I was, so it was fun, but very unsatisfying."

"What else happened?"

I then told her about my shopping trip, meeting Rick, and our trip to Florida. When I got to the part about Derek, I heard her growl on the other end. She didn't want me to skip any juicy parts, so I laid them all out for her.

"He's a pastry chef?" Lora asked. "Yum, I want to get to meet him too."

"And he co-owns a steakhouse next to the hotel, and a bar in Tallahassee, Florida. He's Cuban, and has those Latin looks."

"Oh God, just my type!"

"Yes, he is your usual type. Maybe you should come down and visit?"

"Oh yeah. That afternoon, while I was sitting by the pool, another guy asked me out. I got bad vibes from him though, so I said no. But I thought I would need a date for that night not to be caught out in a lie. So I called Rick. He just happened to have tickets to a Tom Cats show at a bar, which at the time I didn't know he owned, in Tallahassee. So we drove down there for that. Again, an amazing show. I had way too much tequila."

"How far is that from Atlanta?"

"Three hours by car. So we left early in the evening and got there just in time for the first set."

"Did you guys stay down there overnight?"

"No, I insisted on returning because I was too drunk and didn't think a motel room was smart. However, we ended up stopping anyway. Oh, Lora, he's a good lover."

"Details, girl!"

"Mmmm, he kisses wonderfully. Deeply and demanding. He gives wonderful head too. He brought me to an orgasm that knocked me out. Unfortunately."

"You fell asleep? With a Latin lover in your bed? You're right, you were too drunk!"

"I know. But the following morning was sweet. He went out to get breakfast for us. We had a nice, if not steamy talk before getting back on the road. We stopped at his house for him to get changed. We started something up in the shower and were about to have epic sex when his phone rang and his partner was in a panic."

"How far have you gone?"

"We had just started. We were connected. He fit me perfectly too. Oh, what a letdown. He quickly had a cold shower and we left. He dropped me at the hotel and went to work."

"After having a couple of new guys, does this make you feel any differently than you did a month ago? Have you changed your opinion about Mark?" asked Lora. "He's the one that captured your heart."

"I've never been in this spot. Yes, Mark is the one who captured my heart, but I'm still not sure if it's real, you know? I need some sleep. No guys for a while."

"Nonsense!" she said. "Sleeping alone is overrated."

"I agree, it's nice to have a warm body next to you. But I haven't been sleeping!" I cried. "That's the problem!"

"Whiner!" she teased. "You've got three hunks after you and you're complaining. Perhaps I *should* come down and take one off your hands, eh?"

"Can you get away and come down for a weekend?"

"Hmmm, let me work on that one. I'll ask Tori if she can come and stay with the kids 'cause Armand is a bit pissed at me right now."

"What happened?" I asked.

"The usual with him. He gets it into his head that I should be his girlfriend, and when I go out with someone else he gets possessive and jealous. He just won't learn."

"Is there a story there I should hear for educational purposes?" I asked, laughing.

"Yes, and I'll have to be there in person to tell you!" she said.

We talked for another twenty minutes and then said goodnight. I went to eat my grilled cheese. It was cold. No problem, it was plain food, which is just what I wanted. There was still watercress next to it, and pickles and whatnot. But I was hungry now and the cold milk was like silk on my throat.

After eating, I left the tray out in the hall and went to bed with my book. A half hour later, I couldn't keep my eyes open any longer, so I turned out the light and snuggled down into the bed.

I decided to give myself space. Usually, a person has to get space from someone else, but I had to get space from myself. These past few months have been way out of hand. Three guys? *I mean, Falon, what are you thinking?* I needed to remember why I was in Atlanta in the first place. My work had started to suffer due to the long nights and too many parties. So for the next while I decided to focus on the job: no bar, no bands, no late nights.

I haven't spoken to Mark since I told him to leave. I suspected he was waiting for me to break the silence. That would make sense. He had left a message, but with me not answering it I was sure he didn't know what was up right now. *Good.* I was still not finished figuring that out myself.

I had to admit I really missed him though, and wished I could just … what? What did I want? I wanted to talk. I wanted to hear from him—even better, get a visit. I guess a part of me had forgiven him. But there was a larger part of me that needed to talk about all of that.

As much as sex adventures with different men was fun, the one guy who fits just perfectly is the one you crave.

The weather was hot and humid and stormy. We were well into hurricane season at the end of July in the South. So far only the one had come close to us in Atlanta, but I had a bad feeling that my luck was about to change.

12—Going out with Clients

Getting up on Monday, the weather looked nasty. Another hurricane was on a course that could bring it to Atlanta. It was thankfully far enough away that we were not being assaulted by her winds yet.

Maybe it would cause enough trouble here that my evening with this "friend" would get canceled.

Thursday rolled around and no hurricanes were coming to save me. I was up, dressed, and fed in good time. It was probably all the rest I had. I went to sleep early last night. That was different!

I paid particular attention to what I wore today because of this dinner I had been asked to go to. I wore a favorite dress of mine that was forest green. It trussed up my bust nicely, and had a neckline that showed very little cleavage. I liked it because it made me feel sexy and elegant. Plus it was a respectable length and dressy, but business dressy. Paired with a black jacket, it was a smashing outfit.

When I got to the office, Ray saw me walk through the door and waved me into his office. He took one look at me and whistled.

"Nice dress," he commented.

"Thanks. Is it appropriate for this evening?" I asked.

"Yeah, it will do. By the way, he's taking you to The Abbey, a very expensive restaurant downtown."

"Is that significant? Does this change my task for the evening?" I asked him.

"No, simply accompany him to dinner, and make sure he has a good time please," was his answer.

"Define 'good time' please."

"You know, pleasant conversation, sparkling wit."

"So nothing afterward?"

He didn't answer. I didn't like that. He's planned something and he's not telling me. I was suddenly more concerned about this dinner than before.

"What did you agree to, Ray?"

"Nothing, I agreed to nothing. Just that I would provide him with a dinner companion. That's all."

"What time do you want me at your office?" I'm still not comfortable with this.

"Come by around five, please," was the answer.

At my office, a pile of messages waited for me on my desk. Apparently, someone had worked at the office on the weekend. Leafing through the messages I discovered one was from Mark, dated yesterday morning. Ah, that is how Ray knew. Either Caroline had told him about the message, or he had taken it himself. The message said that he was coming into town next week for a presentation by the company. He and Gwen would be there.

Presentation? Hmmm, I wondered what sort of presentation that was? I'd ask Ray when I dropped off the Gantt charts. I set to work uploading the work from the laptop to the network drive and printing out the charts for Ray. It took the better part of a couple of hours to fine tune them and complete the data entry, but when complete it was a stunning picture of how we had underestimated our time!

Just after lunch, I walked down to Ray's office and put the charts on his desk. He wasn't around and neither was Caroline, so they must be out for lunch again. He'd get burned, but I warned him not to play with that fire. Oh well.

At the appointed time, I tidied myself up and went back to Ray's office to meet this client. Most everyone else had already left the office—they started leaving by 4:30—so it was mostly unnoticed that I had this meeting.

When I got there, the gentleman was already there sitting in a chair opposite Ray. As I appeared at the doorway, the two of them stood, and I discovered the client was a shorter man— With my shoes on, I was taller than him. I preferred going out with tall men, but this wasn't a date. It was a business dinner.

"Mr. Warren, this is the talented young woman I've been telling you about, Falon Robertson," introduced Ray, "Falon, this is Kevin Warren from Millateck Industries of Charleston."

"Pleased to meet you, Mr. Warren," I said. "I understand that you are interested in the software we install for process manufacturing."

"Call me Kevin, please, Falon. I've heard some amazing things about you," he said. "I am, but we don't want to talk business all night, surely."

"Whatever you say," I said, glancing at Ray. You never knew what he would brag about.

"Mr. Warren has hired our group to perform the same function we are doing here, for his enterprise in Charleston. That will be our next project, slated to start Q2 next year," explained Ray.

"I look forward to hearing about Millateck, Mr. Warren. We can get a jump on the project over dinner," I said enthusiastically.

"Call me Kevin. I insist. Shall we?" asked Kevin, holding out his arm for me to take.

"Certainly. Ray, I'll see you in the morning, then. Good night," I called back to my boss.

"Have fun, you two!" Ray said, following us out.

I was led down to the garage, where Kevin had a BMW parked. He was acting the perfect gentleman, opening the door for me and handing me down into the seat. The car was quite the luxury vehicle. We drove in relative silence as he was navigating through the traffic. However, I noticed that most of the cars were exiting the city as we were going in. I commented on that as it was odd for me to see an evacuation of a city on a Thursday evening.

"Well, the downtown core is really just office complexes," replied Kevin, "We Southerners prefer to party in our own neighborhoods."

"Montreal, where I'm from, never sleeps. There are always crowds walking the streets, even in the middle of winter."

"Montreal is a city I've always wanted to visit. I've seen photos of it at night and it looks beautiful. But I hate the cold! Brrrr!" he said, shivering just at the thought of it.

"Surprisingly for you, our summers are just as hot—reaching temperatures in the high nineties, and it's humid too. Our summers are just short. We really only get hot weather for about three months."

"Oh really? I didn't know that. Perhaps I shall visit one day, then. When is the best time to visit Montreal?"

"Well, during the summertime there are lots of festivals: the Montreal Jazz Festival, the Blues Fest, and the Just For Laughs comedy festival to name a few. There's always something going on. As well, we host the Montreal Grand Prix if you're into racing."

"I love jazz," said Kevin. "That one would be fine to see, except that I would need someone to accompany me," he said suggestively.

Ignoring his comment, I continued with, "There are lots of open air, free concerts during the music festivals. Thousands of people come from all over to party in our streets all hours of the day. It's quite the spectacle."

"So if I come up for this festival, could I count on your hospitality?" he inquired.

Not sure exactly what that meant, I played it cool. "I can surely recommend good places to stay and eat, of course," I answered.

He seemed a little dissatisfied with my vague answer, but too bad. I wasn't about to promise something to a client I couldn't do. Boundaries, remember?

We continued to the restaurant in silence. When we got there, I saw that The Abbey was just that—a huge ancient church that had been converted into a restaurant. The valet parked the vehicle while we walked into the restaurant. Immediately, you could tell this was an expensive place. The servers were all men, and they were dressed impeccably in black tie. White linen was everywhere, and huge chandeliers hung from the ceilings. The place was so huge that in spite of the crowd, there was hardly any noise—just a dull murmur of voices.

We were shown to a table for two almost directly in the center. Menus were handed to both of us, but mine had no prices. *Oh oh!* In Montreal, that meant pricey. When the man was given the prices and the lady not, the prices were usually very high. I had better be careful what I selected.

Kevin ordered a bottle of Châteauneuf du Pape, and he specified a bottle from 1983—a wine that was usually quite expensive. I was not much of a wine drinker, but I knew that much. So he was trying to impress me. Why? This was not a date. There was not going to be any personal effort on my part. *Hmmm, better watch this carefully. I should have pressed Ray for more details on what he had meant by showing this man a "good time."*

When the waiter came to take our order, I was interrupted.

"Allow me, Ms. Robertson. I know the chef here personally and would be in the best position to suggest their finest dishes."

"Okay, if you wish," I answered. And he continued on, ordering filet mignon with several accompanying dishes. When he was finished, I touched the waiter on the arm and asked him for a glass of water too. He nodded at me and left.

"I'm sorry if I presumed too much, Falon. It's just that I want you to have the perfect experience here," he explained.

"Not at all, thank you," I answered. "So, please tell me about your company, Millateck."

"Ah, let's not spoil this evening with talk of business," said Kevin smoothly.

And all my warning bells went off. Damn! I should have picked up on this earlier. *Watch out, Falon, keep on your game.*

Kevin spent the dinner gently probing me for personal details and steering the conversation back to personal subjects every time I tried to steer it toward business.

"Falon, tell me, how old are you?" he asked.

"That is not something you ask a lady," I answered. I countered with, "Where is Charleston from here?"

"It's east and a little south of Atlanta, on the coast in South Carolina. Charleston is a very old city with a great deal of history," he answered. "So I hear that you are dating the owner of the company?"

"Again, Mr. Warren, not an appropriate question," I answered. "What does Millateck do?"

"I told you I didn't want to talk business," he answered. "Tell me about your family, then."

"I was brought up to do small talk with new acquaintances at a dinner table, Mr. Warren. I do not deem my personal life small talk."

"My, you're testy," he said. "I'm just making conversation. What did you study in school?"

"Is this an interview?" I asked. "I went to McGill University in Montreal. I studied business." Of course, this wasn't quite the truth, but I didn't feel any compulsion to tell this man anything about myself.

"Are you married?"

"Again, not appropriate. I am divorced."

"Then how about sex. Will you talk about sex?" he asked boldly.

"No!" I cried. "I will not talk about that with the 'friend' of my boss, thank you very much."

"Well you should get your sex on while you're in the South," he said. "Do you have a boyfriend at least?"

I really couldn't believe this man. I wanted to shut him down but heard myself telling him the truth as an answer. "No, not at the present. I went through a heartbreak recently, so I'm avoiding that right now."

"Pity," he said. "There's nothing better for heartbreak than to play the field and get well and completely satisfied. I could help with that. Perhaps I could interest you in a little Southern hospitality, Charleston style." He grinned.

"Um, no thank you," I stated simply.

"Come now, Falon, we're both adults. You're a fine-looking woman, and I can satisfy you remarkably well," he boasted.

"Mr. Warren, thank you but I'm not interested," I objected.

"You owe it to yourself to try some fine wine and some fine Southern men. Variety is the spice of life!" he quipped.

I could not believe he used that line!

"Really, Mr. Warren, (I was stressing the mister part), I will not be sleeping with you. That's my final word."

I was getting annoyed.

"Ms Robertson ...

Finally it was becoming less personal.

He continued, " I have spent a great deal of money on you this evening. I expect a reciprocal arrangement."

"Mr. Warren, I am not sure what my boss told you, but I am not a prostitute. I do not trade sex for food for anyone. I am sorry you believed otherwise."

"Ms. Robertson, I do believe you are a cocktease and an insufferable one. Wearing that dress and coming on to me like a hussy!" He was getting red in the face.

At that moment, I spied a figure that was vaguely familiar walking toward our table through the restaurant.

It was Mark! Oh joy! A rescuer! Wasn't I thinking about him just a couple of days ago?

He sat down at the table next to us, putting his back to me but making himself as close as possible. He began reading the menu. *Mark, notice me, please!*

I turned back to the lech sitting across from my table and decided then and there that I would never go work at his company.

Now, how do I get myself out of this night?

"Mr. Warren, where I come from, language such as what you have used is not only rude but offensive. It could also be considered sexual harassment seeing as you are a client of my boss. Where I come from, a man does not admit that he spends lots of money and expects sex in return. Where I come from, a jerk like you would be put in their place. Where I come from, a lady is treated with more respect than you've shown me. Now, if you'll excuse me, I shall leave you to your Châteauneuf du Pâpe and filet mignon and excuse myself from your presence. I never liked that wine!" I said a little loudly.

I was about to get up from the table just then when I felt a hand on my shoulder.

"Ms Robertson, I do believe you need a ride home?" asked a quiet Texan voice behind me.

I looked up to see Mark's face beaming down at me. "Why, Mr. Chisholm, what an unexpected surprise. Thank you, yes, I was just leaving this cad with his bill," I said pointedly.

Kevin stood up and threw his napkin on the table and stood there challenging Mark. Now that was comical! A 5'6" man challenging a 6'3" Texan! Kevin was posturing and puffing up, and Mark just looked down at him with a smile on his face. Of course Kevin thought he had more money than God and that would win the day.

"Southern gentlemen do not treat ladies like that," he said condescendingly. "If what I heard in the last few seconds is any indication, you are lucky Ms Robertson was here this long," he said, turning to me. "After you, ma'am."

With a deep breath, I stood up and marched out of the restaurant and Mark followed. Kevin was still standing at the table, probably humiliated. *I'd better call Ray as soon as I get back to the hotel.* I just couldn't believe my luck! What were the chances Mark would be here to rescue me?

Once we were outside, I turned to him. He was smiling and looking at me.

"I'm so glad you happened to be there!" I breathed.

"I'm glad I was able to help. I didn't like the tone he was taking with you. It was just cheap and uncivilized!"

I stepped toward him and hugged him. After a second's hesitation, I felt his arms wrap around me too. It felt like coming home.

But I was angry with him right now, right? I pulled away.

"I'm still angry with you," I said.

"I know. I'm glad you're safe, though. He would have been a problem," he said. "Can I take you to eat somewhere?"

My stomach growled.

"I am hungry. I never got to eat my meal. Thank you."

"There is a good steakhouse right near your hotel."

"Sounds like a plan."

But when we got there, I knew he meant the restaurant next door, Rick's restaurant. This could get sticky. At least Rick would probably be in the kitchen.

"I've missed you," Mark started once we were seated in a corner booth. "I have been worried about you since our last talk."

"You laid a whole bunch of shit on me, that's for sure," I responded. "At least you still look like Mark. Maybe you could alternate with Zisis and we could have a threesome," I joked.

"I deserve that," he said. "That said, you're safe. The bite won't be dangerous to you. I didn't know this at the time, but there is another 'ingredient' to the equation that didn't happen."

"So no one is turning or dying?" I asked.

"No, not at all," he answered.

"So I have to ask, what is the missing ingredient?"

"Consent. Knowledgeable consent. In the ceremony, where the facts are explained, and the mortal woman gives her consent, then the venom has its full potency."

"Won't that mean that if you bite me now, that's what would happen?" I asked. "Because you have explained it to me?"

"No, because you still have to consent to the ceremony and truly be in love with me."

"Oh. So biting me won't kill me right now?" I smiled. Because I remembered what that bite did to me.

"No, it won't," he grinned, knowing full well what I meant.

We sat in silence for a moment. Mark took my hand on top of the table and squeezed it gently and released me.

Mark, of course, behaved courteously in public. Not a single mannerism out of place. It was a polite, amiable dinner between two business colleagues. Which is what the other dinner should have been but wasn't. The meal was actually very good.

"So how did you know about this place?" I asked.

"Well, it is next door to the hotel you're in," he answered. "But Gwen had mentioned it may be a good investment for us. The chefs are very talented, and they own the place. It's always best to invest in restaurants that are chef owned."

"Oh, why?"

"Because they make the final decisions, and they have their heart invested in its success. Besides, I hear they are up for a James Beard Award."

"The ambiance, the menu, and the food has been wonderful. It's good to get to try the place before you put your money down, right?"

"Yes. That's another reason I suggested it."

Our dishes were cleared, and the waiter suggested the house specialty, mille feuilles for dessert. Mark agreed and we both ordered the French pastry and coffee with Grand Marnier. They were excellent: the pastry was light and flaky, and the custard rich and smooth. The whipped cream was fluffy and perfectly balanced. Well done, Rick!

Of course, I didn't say that out loud.

After we finished our meal, we sat there having our coffee and Grand Marnier—something to be savored slowly. A murmur broke out on the other side of the restaurant with some of the patrons. I glanced up to see the two chefs coming out of the kitchen and walking over to our table. I held my breath.

"Mr. Chisholm, it's an honor to have you dine with us this evening," said Rick's partner.

Rick was looking at me and then back again at Mark. I was not sure what he was thinking.

"How has the meal been?" he asked the both of us.

"It has been remarkable, really," said Mark, "I commend you both on a superb menu, and amazing food. Your presentation is beautiful too."

"Thank you!" gushed Rick's partner. "I'm Justin, and this is my business partner, Ricardo. We're very pleased to be able to serve you."

"Justin, Ricardo, thank you. I'm definitely interested in investing, and my partner Gwen will be in touch." He shook both their hands.

The two chefs bowed slightly and walked back toward the kitchen, stopping now and then to speak to other patrons in the dining room.

"Does Ricardo know you, Falon?" asked Mark after a minute, "I could swear he was looking at you with recognition."

"Well, actually we met in a mall on Saturday. He was shopping for a charity, and we ended up sitting on a bench together," I answered him. "Rick invited me to accompany him to Tallahassee to see the Tom Cats a week ago."

"Did you have a good time?" asked Mark. He was grinning at me.

"Yes, it was a great show. We ended up driving home at 3:00 a.m., though, and Rick couldn't drive safely after an hour. So we stopped at a motel for the rest of the night to get some sleep."

"Oh? Just sleep?"

"There may have been some hanky-panky," I said with a grin. "I was very drunk on tequila."

"I think he has a bit of a crush on you," said Mark. "You did mention a threesome."

"Why? Are you interested?" I teased him. I wasn't sure if I should tell him everything. I still was unsure of where we were as a couple.

"We'll discuss that topic at a later date," he said. "What do you think of him as a businessman?" he asked me.

"Well, I've not met his partner before now, and I'm not sure I have the kind of review you need to assess a business partner," I said.

"Well, you've had a chance to get to know him a bit. Does he strike you as honest?"

"Yes, honest. Perhaps he's a bit shy. Spontaneous, I think. I think he can make decisions quickly. I hadn't expected the invite. It came out of nowhere. He certainly wants to take his restaurant to the top. Oh, and they also own the bar in Tallahassee. He makes mille feuilles just exactly the way they're supposed to be."

"Would you say he takes his business very seriously?" asked Mark.

"I think he's very dedicated to the restaurant. He told me about his training background, and he has the cooking pedigree for sure."

"When Gwen suggested this place, I thought I would come and check it out," he said.

"So how did you end up at The Abbey rescuing me?" I asked him.

"I knew you were in trouble," said Mark cryptically.

"But how did you know where to find me?" I asked again. Then I stopped and remembered. He had that ability like Zisis … because he was Zisis.

"Ah, you remember. Yes, I can sense you, your emotions. I picked up your anger, disgust, and a few other things, and knew I had to be there to make sure you didn't get hurt," he replied softly.

I let it go for now. We were having a nice dinner; I didn't want to get into all that at the moment. A little while later we finished our third cup of coffee and got up to leave. The Grand Marnier had an effect on me, so when I stood the room swirled a bit. Mark noticed and came to my side, grasping my elbow and guiding me out.

When we got to the front door of the hotel, he let go of my arm and turned to face me.

"Falon, I'll drop you off here, okay?"

"Why? Aren't you coming upstairs?" I asked hopefully.

"Yes, but not through the lobby," he said. "I'll meet you upstairs, okay?"

"Okay," I said, a little confused. *What was the difference?*

Walking through the revolving doors into the lobby, I spotted Franco waving at me, so I went to the front desk on my way upstairs.

"Good evening, Ms Robertson, I have some messages for you," he said as he handed over a pile of pink slips.

"Thanks, Franco. I appreciate your effort! Sorry if you are having to be my secretary!" I said.

"No problem, it's my job," he replied. "Have a good evening."

I proceeded to the elevators. Brandon intercepted me on the way.

"Hey, Falon, are you coming to the bar tonight?" he asked hopefully.

I looked at my watch. "I don't think so, Brandon. I'm a little tense right now. I just had a horrible evening with a client."

"What do you mean?" he asked, concerned.

"I'll tell you about it later, okay? I just need to go up and shower and get some of the slime thrown on me washed away."

"Okay, I'll come up afterwards," he said as he walked away.

"No!" I called back, but it was too late.

The elevator doors had closed and he had disappeared into the bar.

Oh my. Well, this won't work, will it? Better get upstairs.

I let myself into my room to discover Mark sitting in the living room with a drink in his hand and his feet on the coffee table. He looked so at home! Mark turned to look at me as I came in.

"Okay, how'd you get in?" I asked.

He walked over to me and took my hands.

"May I hug you?" he asked.

I walked into his arms and he embraced me with the longing of separation. He kissed me thoroughly, making sure no section of my skin was ignored. When he stepped back, his desire showed in his swirling gold irises. His eyes were those wonderful pools of brown. I felt myself getting lost in them again.

"You look amazing tonight, by the way," he said. His voice was rough with emotion. "I'd almost forgotten how beautiful you are."

"Really? I'm not memorable?" I teased. I noticed that he hadn't answered my question.

"Oh, you're memorable alright! Are you sure you're alright after tonight?" he asked me.

"Well, I'm much better now," I said. "Are you staying?"

"Unfortunately, I cannot. I would dearly love to stay with you tonight, but I must be gone soon," he said with disappointment all over his face.

"That's a bummer. I have missed you," I said honestly. "Mark, where does this leave us—all your immortality and such?"

"Well, my position hasn't changed. I'm deeply in love with you. I am hoping you feel the same way. If you do, then we have options."

"I was in love so deeply with Zisis ... and then he hurt me ... split me in two. It took a long time to heal from that. I must admit it was you who stitched my heart back together. Learning that you were Zisis twisted that somehow and I don't know how, and I don't understand what I'm feeling anymore. I see you, but I remember Zisis. I want it to just be you."

"Does it help that Zisis is officially dead?"

"Did he suffer horribly?" I asked with a grin.

"He did. His heart was torn asunder from his body and broken into tiny bits," Mark said.

"That makes me feel better somehow," I said.

"We still have a lot to talk about, and I'm not in a position to be with you quite yet. I have a few issues to resolve on my end," he explained. "When I do come to you, I want you to be clear on what you want."

In spite of all the diversions I'd had, Mark was still the one I wanted to be with. I stepped into his arms again and hung on to him, putting my head against his chest listening to his body. His arms slid around me and I suddenly felt very safe.

"I know what I want," I said.

Again, that familiar feeling that we'd been this way forever, but now I understood why. Ultimately, my body knew who he was even if my eyes hadn't. He rested his head on top of mine and just held me there. Sighing, I melted against him. My body got all soft and mushy.

He picked me up effortlessly and carried me into the bedroom, where he laid me on the bed. My heart started to race.

"We can't tonight. Oh God, I want you so badly right now, but I've got to leave," he said when he knelt in front of me on the floor and gathered me into his arms.

"Not even for a few minutes?" I asked hopefully.

"I don't want just a few minutes with you, Falon. I want a lifetime. I want ten lifetimes," he repeated in a whisper.

He took my face between his hands and kissed me tenderly before he stood up.

"Falon, I will be here for business in a week or so, with Gwen. Hopefully, by then we can sit down and have a long conversation. For now, I've got to leave."

"What am I supposed to do? Just sit and wait for you? Who do you think I am?" I asked, a little annoyed, I think because I wasn't convincing him to stay.

"No! I don't want you to wait for me," he said. "The only way you'll know we are meant for each other is if you are with other men. I will always be here if you need me, if you're in trouble." He looked very serious. "Falon, I love you. I have always loved you."

And then he was gone again. He simply disappeared. I must have blinked or something, because he exited the room without me noticing it. I got up and walked into the other room, but there was no sign of him.

He said he loved me. I would hold on to that.

The more questions I thought of, the more confused I got. Realizing I couldn't solve these mysteries without Mark, I tried to dismiss them from my mind for now. I looked at the clock; it was 9:45. I would call Lora and talk to her about this weekend—but after leaving a message for Ray.

Oh yeah, the other messages.

Retrieving the little pile of pink slips off the coffee table where I'd dropped them, there were two messages from Brandon and one from Rick. No surprise there.

Oh well, these mysteries would have to wait until tomorrow. Tomorrow was Friday—I was going home for the weekend, so I had to pack. Luckily, I didn't have to check out, but I did have to pack all my clothes to take them home to launder. I'd be leaving straight from the office, so I needed to take everything with me tomorrow morning.

The phone rang. It was Lora and we talked about me coming home. We would get together on Saturday. I told her I had new stories to tell her and signed off around 10:30 to finish packing.

With all my dirty clothes packed, I decided to make myself some tea in the room coffee maker. While the water was brewing, I drew a hot bath. That would help me sleep. Scented oils filled the room on the rising steam as I dipped my toes into the water. I slid into the tub with a grateful sigh. Sitting there sipping my tea, soaking away the stress generated by the events of this evening, was heavenly. By the time the water had cooled and my tea was gone, I was ready to sleep.

Not even bothering to put on night clothes, I slipped into bed and curled into a ball and was fast asleep very quickly.

A knock at my door woke me up. Glancing at the clock, I saw it was after two. In my clumsiness, I knocked the receiver off the phone and dove for it on the floor.

Getting out of bed, I went to the door, calling out "Coming!" I grabbed the blanket, wrapping it around me, and looked through the peephole and couldn't see anyone. Thinking they must have left, I opened the door. Brandon was standing there apologetically. He beamed when he saw me.

"I guess I should have called first. But I like the way you answer your door," he said.

"Come in!" I whispered urgently and blushed at the same time. "There's no need to wake up the rest of the floor."

I knew that would be difficult as there were only three or four rooms up here, and they were spaced out really far. I closed the door as he came in and then asked him to wait there a second.

"I'll be right back," I told him.

Walking back into the bedroom, I found my night shirt and put it on before going back to Brandon.

"What can I do for you?"

"May I stay with you tonight?" Brandon asked. "I do know what time it is, and we can just sleep. I am tired." He smiled at me, pausing.

"Um, I was asleep."

"I'm so sorry I woke you up." He walked over to me and wrapped his arms around me.

I hadn't perceived he was almost as tall as Mark and very similarly built. Obviously, I had a type and didn't know it.

He held me there, just as Mark had a little while ago, then picked me up and carried me into the bedroom. I think I might have been asleep again before he laid me down. Although I do have a dreamy memory of feeling his body lay next to mine and holding me.

13—Meet the Nigerians

Home sweet home. God, it was nice to wake up in my own bed with my cats cuddled all around me. My flight last night landed before dinner time, giving me lots of time to spend with them, and one extra night at home.

Today, I was going to see my friends. Hooray! I had woken up slowly, rising to consciousness unwillingly.

Friday morning was interesting. I woke up to find Brandon sound asleep next to me. He too was naked, and the blankets were not covering him. I didn't remember him putting me to bed! In fact, I didn't remember anything after Mark took me home after that disastrous dinner.

Brandon had been lying on his stomach with one leg flung over the edge and his other foot hanging off the end. I noticed his buns were nice! I had caught myself when I had started leaning over to kiss them. Not a good idea. I had to get to the airport. As I tried to get out of bed, I felt his hand grasp my waist, then his arm encircled me and pulled me toward him. As I had tumbled backward and landed on him, he turned me around and kissed me good morning.

"It is very nice to wake up beside you," he said.

"I don't even remember you getting here!" I admitted.

"That's okay, I woke you from a sound sleep, and you fell asleep in my arms. So I picked you up and brought you to bed. Then I joined you. It was very nice just falling asleep next to you too." He smiled.

He started kissing me again and I pulled away, sitting up.

"I'm sorry, Brandon, I just don't have time today. I'm going home for the weekend, and I have to get to the office first and then get to the airport at 10:00."

"Okay. Here, let me help you down with your bags." He got up and dressed, then waited for me while I finished getting ready to leave.

When I was ready to leave, he admired me for a moment, then grabbed my bags and I followed him through the door. Downstairs, he asked me if I needed a cab, and I told him that I would be driving to the airport later. Dropping a kiss on both sides of my face and one on my mouth, he said so long and disappeared through the revolving doors.

I headed for the dining room for breakfast. Janelle was on duty this morning, and she called me over to one of her tables.

"Checking out today, Falon?" she asked when she saw my bags.

"Ah, no, just going home for the weekend. I'll be back on Monday."

"Would you like your usual breakfast today?"

"Yes please!" I answered, pulling my book out of my bag. Just then, Rick came running into the dining room and was looking around. When he spotted me, he came right over to my table.

"Falon, glad I caught you. I haven't had a chance to call you since our Florida weekend, but I didn't want you to think I was avoiding you!" he said, out of breath.

"I didn't, Rick, that's okay. By the way, the mille feuille was done to perfection!" I complimented him.

"Thank you! That means a lot coming from you. Guess what?"

"What?"

"I have been invited to Montreal for a chef's conference!" He was excited.

"Oh, that's wonderful. When?" I asked.

"This weekend. Isn't that great? But I wanted to tell you because I wouldn't be able to see you this weekend. Sorry!" he said disappointedly. "I'm on my way to the airport now, but I was hoping you would be at breakfast, so I stopped by."

Then he noticed my bags. "Oh, you're leaving today?" Now he really looked dashed. "Will you be returning to Atlanta?"

"Not to worry, I'll be back on Monday. Promise," I assured him. For some reason, I didn't tell him I was going home this weekend.

"Oh good. Then I'll be able to cook for you next week ... if you'd be interested in coming over to my house for dinner, that is."

"That sounds like fun," I answered. Then with a little bit of flirting I said, "We can try out that big shower you have again—afterwards, of course."

"Mmmm, I would like that," he said. Suddenly his voice had changed into a sultry Latin steam. "We could try out the blower again too, I think," he said suggestively.

"Mmmm, now I would like that," I said.

He leaned in and kissed me before he was off. It was getting very confusing—three men in one day. *What am I going to do?* Lora would know!

The rest of the morning was uneventful, thankfully. I didn't see Ray before I left, so I didn't get an update about the fallout from the fiasco with Kevin Warren.

All was good. I caught my flight, settled in for a nap, and looked forward to snuggling Mr. Paws and Scooter.

When we had landed in Montreal, it took a while to find my bags and to get the taxis, but I got home by 4:00. The boys were clamoring at the door, and I couldn't give them enough love for at least thirty minutes. I didn't even bother unpacking just yet, but went and sat on my couch with one of them on either side of me. We just sat there, the three of us for a while, as I gazed out the patio doors to the activity outside. The cats went and stretched out in the sunshine, flipped upside down with their paws stretching and "making bread" the way they did when they were ultimately happy. It was a good moment to be content.

They only roused when there was a knock on the door.

"Who is it?"

"Armand."

"Oh, can you come back in say an hour or two? I need to shower and dress."

"I'll see you then."

I was unpacking by the time he knocked again. When he walked in, he smiled in delight that I was home again. He gave me a big hug and sat down to listen to the tales I could tell him. As I was putting the first load of laundry on, he fetched a couple of beers from the fridge, and we went and sat on the balcony.

"So what's Atlanta like?" he asked.

"Hot and steamy! Oh, I got caught in a hurricane!" I told him.

"Really, was it scary?" he asked. So I told him the story about standing on the roof and he scolded me for that. And I told him about seeing the Tom Cats and driving through the rain. He was interested in hearing all about the dancing too. I told him about the scum of a client who tried to buy sex with dinner and Armand got red in the face with anger until I told him I had gotten away from the creep.

I even told him about the jerk at the bar, and that a Southern gentleman had rescued me from the clutches of the uncouth creature. I related that particular story in my best Southern belle voice—with plenty of "I do declares" to spice it up. I had Armand in stitches.

A couple of hours later we'd finished a few beers each and he had to go babysit for Lora again. So I said so long and that it was nice to catch up again. After he left, I changed the laundry around and called Lora.

"So where are you going?" I asked her when she answered the phone.

"Over to your place, of course!" she answered.

"You didn't tell Armand that, did you?"

"Are you kidding? He'd skin me! Get dressed, we're going out!" she insisted.

"Ah, Lora, I want to stay in!" I protested just a bit too much.

"Sure! Right! Next you're going to tell me you've had no sleep all week," she chided me.

"Well, actually…"

"Never mind. I'll be there in fifteen!" She hung up on me! Huh!

What was I going to wear? I went sifting through my home clothes and found jeans and a shirt that were reasonable and clean—back to my usual uniform when going out with Lora. It would be welcome to watch for a change!

True to her word, Lora was ringing my bell fifteen minutes later. By the time she got upstairs I was dressed in clean clothes and my hair was brushed.

"Hey, you're not going out like that. I want that bombshell that's been wandering around Georgia," she said.

"All those clothes are dirty," I said.

"Then let's wash them," she said, pushing me down on a chair. She went rummaging through my clothes.

"Look what I found! You've been holding out on me!" said Lora as she came walking back into the living room dangling a leopard print bra from her fingers. In her other hand, she had the black lace top that I basically tied up in the front.

"Here, put these on," she said.

I stripped out of the tee and bra I was wearing and put on the leopard bra and lace shirt.

"Wow, that is very hot. I like that the bra is a deep-cut demi too. Your nipples are kind of ready to pop out. The lace shirt hides the obvious well. Now those jeans, uh-uh. You're not wearing those."

Lora went back to my room and returned with a pair of black jeans that were lower cut and tighter. I had to pour myself into them, but they looked good. With my midriff bare, my boobs on display, and wearing tight pants and heels, I was apparently ready to go "cock shopping" as Lora put it. I was worried I would get propositioned.

With a sigh, I led the way down to my car. My jeans were hurting me as I sat down, but I knew they would loosen up once I started dancing. We headed out for our favorite spot—the Peel Pub. There we had our usual spaghetti dinner and a pitcher of beer.

After we had finished eating, we sat back into our ritual of picking out the worst and best dressed, as well as the losers and winners of the crowd. I was surveying the men at home, and I had to admit, at this place there were lots of good-looking black guys. One in particular was ogling me. I ogled back. We smiled at each other.

"I've got a good vibe coming from that one," Lora said, pointing to one of the handsome black guys at the table I happened to be watching.

"The guy in the snazzy black shirt?" I asked.

"Yeah, and the one next to them. I am picking up really good energy from them."

"Is that your supernatural self speaking or the horny woman?"

"A little of both, but my witchy side is drawn to those two for some reason"

"Well, let's dance on over there and see if they are as good a catch in person."

Lora and I got up and moved to the dance floor where we were getting our groove on. Within a few minutes, both of those handsome guys had come over to us and were dancing alongside. Having a conversation on a dance floor is near impossible, but there are ways to communicate. Mr. Black Shirt was up against my body and we were swaying to the music together. There was definitely a rhythm to us. When I put my hands on his shoulders, his naturally went around my waist.

"Would you like to sit down? he asked when the music was interrupted for a minute.

"Yes, come this way." I led him to our table.

"My name is Tarence."

"Falon, nice to meet you," I said. "You have an interesting accent. Where are you from?"

"Nigeria. My brother and I are here for school."

"What are you studying?"

"I'm in architecture, he's in engineering." He replied, as he moved closer to me on the bench.

I could feel the heat between us. The side of my body was tucked under his arm because he had put his arm across the back of the bench. Lora returned to our table with another.

"This is Will," introduced Lora.

"He's my brother," said Tarence.

They both sat on the other side. The four of us chatted for a while about Montreal and school and all kinds of things. They guys got up to get their things from the other table. It gave Lora and I a minute to confer.

"Well?" I asked.

"Really good karma on these two. I am getting a really strong sense of good."

When Tarence got back he asked me to dance again, I agreed, and we took to the dance floor. He was a very good dancer and we had a lot of fun.

When we got back to our booth, Lora was on Will's lap. She was enjoying herself just a tad too much.

Tarence and I slipped into the opposite side. As soon as I was beside him, he nuzzled me on the neck and asked if he could kiss me. When he reached over I leaned into the kiss. He pulled me over so that I was sitting on his lap. This made the kissing easier. I felt him slip a hand under my shirt and gently caress the side of my breast. When he buried his nose between my breasts an involuntary moan escaped from my lips, and when I could feel his arousal coming on under me, I heard a moan escape from him too.

"Falon, would you like to come back to my place?" asked Tarence. "I have a hot tub on the roof, with a view of the city that is unparalleled. We could have a nice party up there."

"Mmmm, that sounds like some good fun. Let me ask Lora."

Lora was on the dance floor with Will doing a raunchy slow dance. I went and spoke in her ear.

"I've been invited Tarence's place to use his hot tub."

"Will, shall we go with them?" asked Lora.

He scooched her in very close so their hips were practically joined and responded, "Ya mama, I certainly would. Especially since my brother and I share an apartment."

I walked back to where Tarence was and indicated we were all in for the hot tub. He got up and took my hand and led us all out of the pub. Out on the street, it was a beautiful night.

"Our place is about three blocks from here," he said. "I'm on Fort just below de Maisonneuve." He wrapped his arm around my waist as we walked down the street.

Will wrapped his arm around Lora too.

"This is going to be an interesting night," said Lora. When we got to the building, we all took the elevator to the twenty-fifth floor. Anticipation was growing as we went up.

"I have something special to show you. Will you trust me?" Tarence asked me when the door opened.

"Yes, I suppose so," I answered.

He took us to the roof, and then outside.

"It is high up, are you afraid of heights? I will keep you safe. But you need to trust me," he said.

"Only falling from heights. I trust you," I responded.

He led us around the corner of the belvedere, which is the building that encloses the top of the elevator. There was a ladder going up to the top. We stopped in front of the ladder.

"Will you trust me?" he asked again.

"Yes," I answered him.

He stood behind me and placed his arms on either side of me on the rungs of the ladder. Then told me to go up.

"Don't worry, I've got you. You won't fall," he said.

We climbed up about twenty feet and reached the top of the belvedere. He helped me off the ladder and held me as I stood up. He walked me to the edge of the building then and showed me my city from a place I would never have dreamed of seeing it.

Will and Lora followed us up the ladder and the four of us stood there.

"It's beautiful," I gasped. "I've never seen my city quite like this before."

"I knew there was something special about these two," Lora whispered to me.

"I like to come up here to be alone to think," said Tarence. "Will just brings girls up here for fun."

"I'm down with that," Lora chimed in. She was standing in front of Will, and he had his arms wrapped around her to keep her warm. It wasn't cold, but you know.

I felt Tarence's eyes on me. He took my hand firmly as I leaned over a bit to look down. He jumped at me and grabbed me around the waist. We stood there for a few minutes, his arms around my waist looking out at all the lights. The building we were on was not one of the tallest in the city. But at twenty-five storeys up, you still had a magnificent view. The office towers like Place Ville Marie were much taller but they were behind us.

"Are you okay?" he asked me.

"Yeah, I'm fine. Exhilarated actually. This is amazing," I said quietly in awe.

"You're not scared?" he asked.

"Not at all. Thank you for bringing me up here!"

We stepped back from the edge and he went and sat down, dangling his legs over the side. I joined him on the rooftop.

"This is a very special place," said Lora. "Where is the hot tub?"

Will smiled and led her back down the ladder. I heard them murmuring together.

"That has got to be the sexiest outfit I've ever seen. We don't need to go swimming just yet, do we?" asked Tarence.

"I don't think so," I said.

He turned me around so that he was shielding me from the general view. His hand was sliding up my leg to my ass and grabbing it.

"I love your ass," he said. "A real woman has curves, nice round curves. I love a big round ass. It gives me something to grab and push into." Tarence buried his nose in my cleavage and inhaled my perfume deeply.

When he raised his eyes to me, I could have sworn they looked a little high. I knew what effect the perfume had on men, especially if they licked it.

"You smell so good." He slid fingers inside my bra and teased my nipples until they were outside of the bra entirely. Taking off my shirt, he bent down and sucked on first one nipple, then the other, nipping and licking them until they were both erect and tingling with need.

After unzipping my jeans, he slid his hand down the front and cupped my mound, sliding his finger into my flower and rubbing my nub until I was squirming under his caresses.

"Come on, I've got a cosy spot for us below." He led me back down the ladder to a spot on the other side of the roof where he had spread blankets and pillows. He knelt down and drew me down beside him. Slowly he undid the zipper again and pulled off my jeans. He was pleased to see no underwear to impede him. He made me lay back so he could bury his nose in my clit and kiss me gently, pulling on the skin and sucking the nub. I almost climaxed right there.

Two fingers started to fuck me while he was sucking on my nub. His fingers were long and thick, giving me a lot of feeling, but it only made me hungrier.

Just when my hips were about to start their own dance, he pulled out his fingers and let go of my nub.

"Go down on me, woman," he commanded.

He helped me sit up. His cock was straining against his jeans. As I undid the zipper, he groaned in relief and he sprang free. He was very well endowed. I took hold of his cock, moving my hands up and down his wonderful shaft. He closed his eyes in pleasure, and moaned a little.

He stood up, bringing his cock to my eye level. I still had my hands wrapped around his member, so now I licked his head and he shivered. His head produced a drop of liquid that I sucked off with my lips. He danced in my hands. As I wrapped my lips around the head, he started twitching, but when I started moving him in and out of my mouth, scraping my teeth along the underside of his head, he screamed in pleasure. He tried to push farther into my mouth than I could handle, which resulted in me withdrawing him quickly.

"What happened?" he asked. "Are you okay?"

"Yes, fine," I said. "I unfortunately have a very sensitive gag reflex, and with well-endowed men I cannot take much in my mouth."

"Oh, that's too bad."

I smiled up at him. "But I have an extraordinarily long vagina, built exactly for guys like you."

"Oh, that's good," he smiled back.

"Agreed."

"Now, isn't that a nice surprise," I overheard Will say to Lora. "You mean to tell me you've been gyrating on that floor without panties all night?"

"Uh huh," she answered.

"Jeez, I wish I had known that!" he said as his voice started to thicken with arousal.

"You do now," she said simply.

In a different corner of the roof, laid out on a blanket, the two of them were having a private affair.

"Do you bring women here often?" I asked.

"No, but I like to be ready. When you go out at night, you never know if you will meet someone who will turn you on enough to want to bring home."

He sat down on the blanket beside me again, and pushed me back against the ground. He took my mound with his hand probing not so lightly. I could feel him getting very excited again.

"Woman, you have a beautiful ass and a beautiful big pussy too. I love it."

He grabbed my ass and encouraged me to lift it up so he could slide his fingers between my cheeks. He slipped his finger inside my back door, which made me gasp. I involuntarily rolled my hips forward. That put me in the direct line of his cock. He moved his cock to my vagina and nestled against me. He groaned when he came into contact with my wetness. As I moved he groaned with excitement. I pressed myself onto his head, slipping him inside.

"Ah fuck that's nice, woman."

He tried pulling out and groaned louder when I squeezed him, keeping him inside. His response was to wiggle his finger, sending some very interesting sensations traveling through me. We teased each other like that for a minute when he took a deep breath and thrust fully inside, gasping as he became one with me.

"Woman, you fit me like a glove, this is nice."

He stopped for a minute, I held him in place and let him feel the breadth and length of me.

My leg involuntarily lifted as I placed it over his hip to give him better access. His body was pinning me against the floor, his cock acting like a dowel joining two objects. He kissed me with hunger as we laid there conjoined. His tongue re-enacted the fusing of our bodies.

One of his hands decided to explore my breasts. He took his fingers, still damp from my juice, and slid them up and down between my breasts. He slid his whole hand inside my bra and drew out the breast from the demi-cup, exposing the nipple above the lace.

Leaning down, he first kissed, then sucked on the nipple, teasing it into an erection of its own.

Up to this point, I had done nothing but lay there.

"I'm going to cum all over you if I don't take a break," he said, chagrined.

"Oh, don't do that just yet."

"You fit me fine, woman. I love how my cock fills you. And your pussy is nice and wet. He had pulled out of me and was kneeling with his erection on full display. I was completely exposed at this point, but no one was there watching.

"Come here, big boy." I motioned for him to get closer.

"I want you to take me from behind."

"It would be my pleasure." I rolled over onto my knees and presented him with my ass.

Tarence moaned at the sight of me. He bent over and gave my slit a sensual lick from clit to anus. Using fingers and tongue, he probed and touched me until I was gasping for him.

"Tarence! Fuck me."

He brought his penis in contact with my vagina. He had swollen even more. He rubbed himself in my fluids to lubricate himself well before he pushed into me.

My coil tightened so quickly I was left breathless as a climax overwhelmed me and exploded through my nether regions like never before.

Tarence waited for the shudders in my body to subside.

"Do you want to continue?"

Oh my God, yes!"

He continued rocking in and out bringing both of us to climax. The two of us were screaming out in ecstasy as we released together. I could feel him pouring his seed deep into me as his cock twitched and danced.

Over the noise we were making, I was surprised to hear Lora and Will having an equally good romp.

We still hadn't been in the hot tub!

Tarence was very careful to not move right now, I believe because he'd softened. He just stayed there inside me, his head deeply inside.

"Did you tip me?" I asked.

"Did I what you?"

"Hit the end of me?"

"Ah, I'm not sure," he said. "Does that do something for you?"

"It surely does. Did you know there is a g-spot at the very end of a vagina next to the opening of the cervix? It's rarely talked about, because most women don't experience it."

"Huh, I did not know that," he said. "It is something I can strive toward. What did you call it? Tipping?"

"Yeah, I got that from someone."

"Did he tip you?" asked Tarence.

"Yes, he did. Does that make you competitive?"

"It certainly does. I consider myself a very good lover." He grinned at me. "I won't be outdone."

Tarence disconnected and curled up behind me. It was a very warm summer night, and the stars were out. Up on the roof it was cooler than on the ground, and the breezes were drying the sweat on my skin. As a result, I had goosebumps everywhere.

"Your skin is pebbling in the breeze," he noticed as he was playing with my nipples, which were indeed "pebbling" and erect. He leaned over and sucked on one of them. I was watching his skin on mine, which I hadn't even thought of before, but it was interesting to see the dark blue-black skin contrasting against my white skin. It was erotic. Seeing his black penis inserted into my white skin was erotic too. Thinking about it got me all aroused again.

"Hmmm, I can smell your arousal again. What were you thinking about?"

"I was envisioning your beautiful black skin penetrating my pale white skin, and I found it extremely erotic."

"It is," he agreed. "I like parting the flesh of a white girl with my cock. The contrast is very erotic to see." And he took his hand and slid three fingers inside me and moved them around to cause my arousal to increase.

"Shall we go use the hot tub?" I asked.

"Are we finished here?" he asked.

I didn't think we were. I was right, as he got between my legs and brought himself into position again. He dipped his head inside me again, to judge the wetness.

"Oh, you're so slick and wet. I love that. It gets me so hard. Your pussy is ready to fuck again." Without warning, he pierced me again with his cock. This time he was aiming for that well-hidden g-spot. As he pounded into me driving as deeply as he could, he had to support his weight over me with his arms, so I opened up my legs as wide as they could go. His thrusts were so forceful his balls were banging into me and the sound of them slapping my ass was almost comical. I almost laughed except his cock had reached the end of my vagina.

"Oooh, my, there it is," I moaned.

"Am I tipping you yet?" he asked hopefully.

"Yes," I answered as his cock hit the end of me. The pleasant pain that accompanied the sensation shook through me as my body quaked with every push.

Tarence took note of the reaction my body had as he tipped me too. I could tell he was learning something from this.

"I like what this does to you," he said huskily. "This level of penetration brings a new level to the arousal. Thank you for showing me this."

"There are positions that enhance this too," I mentioned.

"Such as?" he asked with a smile.

I explained clinically: "Me on my knees in a downward dog. It angles my vagina so that you hit the back wall, and your curve will rub that wall all the way in. Putting exquisite pressure on both the cock and vagina."

"Let's try," he said, eagerly. After another deep thrust, he stilled a second, holding himself deep inside. As he twitched, his head rubbed that spot and sent me into yet another climax, only this one was long and drawn out as the quaking became shudders that emanated out from that point like ripples in a pond.

He held his position while the climax took me. He rode it with me, seeing all the sensations show on my skin and face. While he watched, his own arousal matched mine, but he did not climax. He pulled out and flipped me over. I went into the downward dog and he again pushed into me.

"Oh fuck, ahhhhh oh my God, ah geez, ahhhh," he cried out as his cock was squeezed down the canal. "Woman, you know your body. This is exquisite. Hold on, I'm going to ride you hard."

Tarence took hold of my ass and rode me hard all right. He relished in the angle my vagina was forcing his penis into, and the depth that he could go. Each time he tipped me, we both felt the collision, and the shudders went through both of us. This time, his release was far more energetic; his cock shuddered with the effort.

We both collapsed on the blanket. He was on top of me, spent, lathered, and smiling.

Fine beads had pooled between my breasts. Small rivulets of water were running down my body and his, pooling on the blanket under us.

He leaned over and kissed me—something he hadn't done much of. The kiss was intimate and deep. It wasn't foreplay this time, but a tender moment sharing an experience.

Will came up behind Tarence and spoke to him.

"Hey, bro, give the lady some privacy," Tarence called.

"Sorry, why don't you two join us in the hot tub?" Will asked, turning around.

"Don't bother turning, Will, we'll all be naked in the tub," I said.

"We'll be right there, Will," said Tarence. I could hear the strain in his voice as he was holding in laughter. He was buried inside me up to his balls and covering up all my parts too.

Tarence and I broke out giggling at that point. We took a few minutes to calm down, and to let his penis retract a little.

"So are you stuck?" I asked.

"Apparently. You, sexy lady are keeping me up. I apparently can't get enough of you. This is a first for me. It's a problem I didn't expect. But oh God, how I love being inside you," he said huskily.

It took ten minutes before my vagina released him enough and he had shrunk enough to slide out. We then walked over to the tub. Tarence had some large beach towels ready to use. Since we were all naked, I didn't worry about wearing a towel. Lora was already in the hot tub already naked, and so was Will.

"Ahh the water is wonderfully hot!" I exclaimed.

Tarence was right behind me, sitting on one of the shelves. "Yes, it's nice. We keep this going all year long. It's really nice when we come up here in the winter. Sinking yourself under the water when it's cold and snowing is a beautiful experience."

Tarence took my hand and pulled me over to his lap. As I sat on him, I felt his cock slide into place. I had never sat on a guy with my back to him while having sex. This again was another interesting position. It let his shaft rub up against that lovely g-spot just inside in the front. He wasn't doing anything, just being inside me.

My attention was momentarily diverted to Lora; she was floating on the second shelf facing me. Will was standing behind her and I could see that he was well endowed too. We all got a glimpse of his erection proudly standing out of the water before he slid into the water behind Lora.

Tarence was doing things to me again. I could feel him inside me, and he was deep. I rotated around his penis without disconnecting us, just swiveled around on him. That sent a few sensations through both of us. Once I was facing him, I could sit down on him more, pushing him deeper inside of me. He liked that. He grabbed both my breasts and tweaked, kneaded, and tugged on them. I started rocking back and forth to move him up against my g-spot.

The water started sloshing everywhere as the four of us got more active. As our climax built up, Tarence got larger, and the larger Tarence got, the more I drove him into me. We climaxed shortly after Lora and Will. It was unavoidable, being witness to it. In some way, having another couple there was more erotic.

"Well, that was a lot of fun," said Lora. "Let's switch."

"Oh!" said Will and Tarence at the same time.

"Are you ladies up to that?" asked Tarence.

"Absolutely," I said.

"Beer and wine," said Will.

"Let's do beer," I said. Lora agreed. The guys got out, threw some towels around their hips, and went in search of beverages.

"Falon, this was a smash!" said Lora when the guys were out of earshot.

"I had fun. Tarence was good. He was nicely endowed too. I saw that Will was as well."

"Oh yeah. He filled me up proper, he did." Her Irish lilt, which had lessened over the night, was coming out again. It ebbed and flowed with her moods.

"I wonder what time it is?" I asked.

"Time to sleep, I fear," she said.

The guys came back a few moments later.

"Tarence, did you happen to notice the time?" I asked.

"Yes, it's 3:40 a.m.," he answered. "Do you need to be somewhere?"

"Asleep," I said.

"Me too," said Lora.

"Well, come with us, then," said Will. They gathered up our belongings, wrapped us in big fluffy towels, and led us to their penthouse apartment. It was a beauty, with at least two bathrooms and two bedrooms. They were nicely separated, one on each end of the apartment too.

I curled up on the big fluffy bed, and Tarence got in and spooned me from behind. I think I was asleep in a matter of minutes.

14—Comparing Notes

Five thirty in the morning brought sunshine spilling across the pillow and waking me up.

When I opened my eyes, I was a little disoriented at first.

Where am I? Oh yeah, penthouse, Nigerians, excellent sex, Lora, were the thoughts that came back to me, in that order. As my consciousness started to include my body, I could feel taut, warm flesh up against mine. I looked under the blankets to see this well-muscled black arm across my body, his hand cupping one of my breasts like a teddy bear.

That was cute.

Now that I was awake though, my body demanded I go pee. I needed to extricate myself from the arm and roll out of bed. It happened to be a king size, which meant it was a long way from the middle to the edge.

I found a bathroom ensuite and finished up. But then I got the urge to explore before going back to bed. Apparently, Lora was on the same schedule as me, because I ran into her in the kitchen.

"Morning," she said to me as I was coming around the corner as quietly as I could.

"Well, that was a night to remember," I said.

"Was, and the rooftop experience was new for me too," she said. "Great sex, nice guys, beautiful home. Wow, we got a trifecta last night."

"Want some coffee?" I asked.

"Maybe. I was just poking around before going back to bed," she said. "Are you staying up or going back to bed too?"

Looking at the time: "I'm going back to bed."

I walked quietly back to the bedroom and carefully lifted the blankets to slide beneath.

"Good morning, beautiful," came a quiet voice from under the covers.

"Oh, I'm sorry I woke you. I just needed to pee."

"That's quite alright. Come here, woman, and I'll warm you up," said Tarence.

I slid to the middle and he pulled me right into his body. He was wonderfully warm.

"Oh! You're freezing!" he cried out. I giggled until I felt his fingers penetrate my vagina and rub me the right way.

"Oh my," I groaned. "That feels nice."

His fingers started moving in and out faster. He added another, and the sensations intensified. I rolled my head over to look at him and he kissed me deeply while another hand cupped my breast.

I twisted my hips so I was on my back, and draped my leg over his hip. This gave him full access to me. His mouth took a breast while his four fingers were slowly fucking me and getting me very, very wet.

He slipped my leg off his hip and moved himself on top of me. When he penetrated me, a deep sigh escaped my lips, followed by a moan as he slid all the way to the end of me and stopped.

"Mmmm, that is sooo good," I murmured. "You feel good inside me."

"You are nice and tight this morning. Last night I stretched you out."

"I could get used to this," I said, smiling. "Do you want a girlfriend?"

What? What was I saying?

"I can't have a white girl as a girlfriend, not seriously anyway," he answered me.

"What?" my eyes snapped open. "What does that mean?"

"My parents wouldn't accept you as a wife. Only a Nigerian woman. My wife has already been chosen for me," explained Tarence sadly. "I am supposed to be married when I return home to Nigeria next summer."

"And what if you fall in love before that?" I asked.

"I could fall for you, Falon. You encapsulate everything I desire in a woman. But I would have to break our hearts."

At this point he had stopped moving and had pulled out. The turn this conversation took had literally deflated him.

"I'm sorry I ruined this for us," I said. "I hadn't realized my question was so loaded."

"It's not your fault," he said. "We work well together, and it's a natural progression."

"Is Will in the same bind?"

"Yes, he is expected to marry whoever is chosen for him too."

"Tough culture," I said. "For now, how about we just cuddle and be with each other?"

"That sounds nice," he agreed. With that, we slid together and spooned, falling asleep in each other's arms.

Lora woke up about two hours later and came and got me.

"Falon," she whispered. "Falon, wake up. I need to get home."

Cracking open an eye, I saw her and knew we needed to leave. "Okay, I'm up."

We dressed quickly and I left a note for the brothers. Running back to the car, which was only a couple of blocks, Lora said she wanted to get home before her kids woke up. I don't know how she did it—because she had a two-year-old who didn't sleep much during the day. I dropped her off twenty minutes later. We hugged and promised to talk again before I returned to the South.

I got back to my apartment by 8:30 a.m. I went back to bed. Mr. Paws was already there, and Scooter was curled up on my pillow. Without disturbing them, I curled up on one side without pulling down the blankets, and the three of us slept till noon.

I woke up to the phone ringing. It was on the other side of my bed, so I had to get up to get it. It was my mom. They were back in Montreal and were wondering if my flight home had been okay. They invited me over for dinner tonight and I accepted. I wanted to hear about their holiday in Florida too.

Armand made another appearance after that. He hung around for an hour or two having a coffee, then trundled off back across the hall. I was still trying to get my laundry finished, and was on my third load when the phone rang again.

I had to run to get it in the kitchen. Picking up the receiver and breathlessly saying, "Hello," into it got an unusual response.

"Oh, I may have the wrong number, sorry." Then silence. I hung up and waited because chances were the person was going to call back, and they did.

"Hello," I answered again.

"Is Falon Robertson there, please?"

"Speaking," I said.

"Hi, it's Rick, Rick Benal ... from Atlanta?" he said with a question in his voice.

"Hi, Rick, where are you?" I glanced at the phone for the number.

"I'm downtown Montreal, actually. I just got out of one of the seminars I was attending, and I was thinking about you. I remembered you said you were from Montreal, so I took a chance looking up your phone number. I was going to leave a message for you."

"That's nice. How's the seminar going?" I asked him.

"It's going great. I've learned a lot and made some good connections here. But you're home! You didn't tell me you were coming home."

"No, but you didn't ask, and I was kind of asleep at the wheel Friday morning," I said.

"I have the rest of today off. Can we get together?" asked Rick.

"Oh, I dunno, Rick. It's Sunday, right? I've got to clean all my clothes and repack them because I fly back tomorrow morning," I said.

"What time is your flight?"

"I've got a 5:30 a.m. flight tomorrow. It's the one I always take."

"That's the one I'm on. Maybe we can get seats together," he suggested.

"That would be cool," I answered sincerely. "I would like that."

"I'll be at the airport by 4:00 a.m., I think. Should I wait for you somewhere?"

"Yes, wait for me near the baggage check."

"Okay, see you tomorrow, then!" he said excitedly.

"Bye."

I looked at the clock, it was 12:45. I had to finish my laundry and get all my clothes packed again. I was about three-quarters finished. One more load to do. While I was making myself some coffee the phone rang again. It was Lora.

"Great news, girl. I have made arrangements to come down to Atlanta next weekend. I'll take a flight down on Friday and come home on Sunday. Sort of what you do, only reverse. We'll have two nights to paint the town Montrealaise!"

"That's fantastic. You can stay in my room, of course."

"That is where I was planning on sleeping—unless I get a better offer," she giggled.

"Hey, I've got two whole rooms, so you can still stay with me. Besides, we might have more fun that way," I said.

"Ow! We're getting naughty now, are we?" Lora chuckled.

"Perhaps. But I gotta go and finish my laundry. I'll call later, okay?"

"Good. Bye."

Checking the clock, I saw it was 2:30. I still needed to shower, change, eat, and get the last load of clothes folded and packed. I might bring some other things down with me too. If I pushed through, I would get everything done and have time to pick up some more cat food for the boys. But I couldn't dawdle anymore.

By 3:30, I had everything done.

I drove over to my parents' for an early dinner. It was good to be home. My mom's place is even more home that mine. We hugged and talked, and the cooking was amazing as always. She rarely cooked fancy food, but whatever she cooked was perfect. I don't remember her ever spoiling something. There was never an overcooked dish or a burnt sauce.

Around 8:30 I said goodnight and went back to my place. I grabbed myself a cold drink of milk, watched a little TV, and went to bed early. A boring—happily—Sunday night.

My alarm clock rang obnoxiously at 3:30 a.m. After smashing my hand on it to silence it, I dragged myself out of bed.

Thankfully, I was smart yesterday, and everything was done. All I had to do was dress and call a taxi. Hopefully, the rest of the day would go just as easy.

When the taxi dropped me off at the airport, I was exactly on time. There was plenty of time to drop off my bags and pick up something to take on the plane. I should be able to find Rick with reasonable ease.

When I got to the bag check area, there he was. He had already checked his bags, so he helped me manhandle mine onto the conveyor belt. Ten minutes later, we were walking to the gate with coffees and snacks in our hands. The person at the desk was able to seat us together so we would be able to chat about our weekends and the trip ahead.

At last, the plane was leaving, and we had the row to ourselves, so we stretched out a bit. Rick encouraged me to lean on his shoulder, and soon I was snoozing up against him. The flight attendant woke me up when they came around for food and drinks. I had ended up with my head in Rick's lap, and he was running his fingers through my hair.

"Oh, I'm sorry, Miss," said the flight attendant. "Would you like any food or drinks during your flight?"

"Yes, please," I answered, and sat up.

"So would I, please," answered Rick. We sat together having our drinks and food quietly.

"That was nice," Rick said.

"Mmmm, what was?" I asked.

"Having your head in my lap while you slept," he said.

"Oh, sorry about that," I answered.

"It's quite alright. I liked it," he smiled.

When we landed, we grabbed a taxi together and drove to the hotel. Rick had left his car at the restaurant on Friday morning, so it was convenient for him to do so. At the hotel door, after the taxi had left, he hesitated, then took my hand.

"It was really nice having you as a flying companion. I had fun talking to you," he said.

"Yeah, it was nice for me too. I'm usually flying alone all the time."

"Can I see you tomorrow?" Rick asked.

"Maybe, but I'll have to find out what is happening at work first. Sometimes there are surprises waiting for me when I get in on Mondays."

"That I understand!" said Rick emphatically. "I'll call you then, mid-afternoon? Can I have your office number?"

I gave him my business number. We kissed and then I went into the hotel. Franco was at the desk again and he saw me come in with my bags. He waved again, but this time there were no messages. I dropped my luggage in my room and got up to the office by 10:00. My day dragged on and I was glad when it was time to leave. I got back to my hotel by 6:30 p.m. and I was bagged. Get an early night, Falon!

When the door of the room closed behind me, I finally sighed. Quiet. At last.

"Falon," came a familiar voice from the bedroom.

15—Public Spectacles

"Hello?" I asked. Who could be here? I walked cautiously into the room, looked around and couldn't see anyone. Thinking I was in the middle of some bizarre joke, I poked my head around the doorway of the bedroom to see if there was someone there.

I still couldn't see anyone, so I went over to the light switch and flipped on the light. There was Brandon, lying prone on my bed, naked.

"Oh, it's you," I said, not quite smiling, "I was wondering who was in my room. How did you get in?" I asked.

"Easy. I asked Franco. It is very useful to be well-known by the hotel staff. I told him I was planning on surprising you with a gift. So he agreed to let me in."

"Hmmm, I'll have to speak to him about this," I commented.

Brandon pouted a little, in a sexy, sensual way. Then he patted the bed beside him to motion for me to join him.

"Not yet, I have to unpack my clothes so they have a chance to de-wrinkle before I have to wear them," I said.

"I'll help."

"No."

I couldn't help myself, I was seething with rage. All while we were putting my clothes away, I just wanted to yell at him. I felt really violated with finding him there without my permission. I could tell he thought it was romantic to be waiting for me, but it was creepy.

"No," I said again. "Brandon, you cannot just let yourself into my room. It's creepy and I don't find it sexy. It feels more like a violation of my privacy."

"I'm sorry, I was trying to surprise you."

"I understand that. Coming up here and knocking is one thing, but letting yourself in is an entirely different thing. You don't have that right. Besides, I don't want the hotel staff to be privy to my private life, thank you very much."

"Sorry, I didn't realize it was creepy. I'll leave you to yourself." He quickly dressed and left.

Once he was gone, I breathed a sigh and got myself unpacked. I liked Brandon, he was fun to hang with, but this was not fun. Now I could get a good night's sleep.

And a little voice in the back of my head whispered, *Hypocrite!' You had no problem with Mark letting himself in.*

Yeah, well, that was Mark and I'm pretty sure he didn't ask the hotel to let him in. I don't know how he got in, but it was not with a key..

The following morning, I got up and got dressed quickly. I was ready to leave in five minutes. When I got to the main lobby, Franco smiled secretly at me, which was exactly what I was afraid of. I went for breakfast in the dining room before I left.

Once at the office I went about the daily exercise of work. Meetings, calls, and follow-ups took up most of my time. Progress reports were required by the client and Ray.

Around 11:00, Ray came into my office and told me that the client had requested a conference sometime this week. They wanted an update on the project. Okay, I would get that prepared. I apparently had three days to prepare for my presentation.

"Ray, did you hear anything from Kevin Warner after he took me out for dinner?" I asked.

"No, I haven't," he said. "Did everything go okay?"

"It depends on how you describe *okay*," I said. "He got very rude and flat out told me he expected sex in exchange for the dinner."

"Really?" asked Ray. "I'm sorry for that."

Somehow I didn't believe Ray. "Well, I got rescued from dinner, so nothing happened. In fact, I dumped him at the beginning with the bill."

"Who rescued you?"

"None of your business, really," I said. I didn't appreciate his apparent lack of concern for the position he had put me in.

"Huh," said Ray as he left the office.

I didn't know if it would be just Gwen or Mark as well at this conference. Mark had told me that he didn't have anything to do with the operation of this company, but maybe he would be there as a partner anyway. Perhaps it would be a bunch of people, I didn't know. I did know that I had to put together a ten-minute presentation on my portion of the project.

Thursday rolled around and it was the day of the conference. The client was due in about thirty minutes. I decided to go and make sure I looked business-like. I had put on a women's business suit. It was a beautiful shade of peacock blue, and had deep marine blue stitching on it for accent.

The jacket was single breasted but buttoned up under my bust, framing my breasts tightly and pushing them together. I wore a white V-neck blouse that was deep enough to show a little cleavage but not scandalous. The skirt was a straight skirt and about four inches higher than my knees. The skirt was sufficiently tight that I decided to wear a thong to prevent lines from showing. I was wearing a really nice pair of navy-blue pumps that had three-inch heels to go with the suit. All in all, I thought I looked smashing.

We all started filing into the conference room. Ray sat me at the end of the table closest to the door. Mark came in with Gwen. This was the first time I was meeting his sister and business partner. She was stunning: beautiful red hair, full lips the color of blood, blue eyes, and creamy white skin. She was slight of build, but full of hips and bust too. She looked like a Barbie doll.

Mark was stunning too. His skin, tanned a deep bronze, offset his brown eyes and dark hair. He was dressed impeccably in a designer suit. Clothes just seemed to drape on his frame perfectly.

They were accompanied by two colleagues from their business. The four of them sat across the table from me, with Mark directly opposite at the end of the table.

Gwen stood and gave a brief introduction. Their group had recently purchased the concrete plant that was installing our software; "our" being the company I worked for in Montreal. The Montreal software developer was hired by the engineering firm Ray worked for to customize the software for the cement plant. It was a three way customer/client relationship. Once that picture was as clear as mud, Ray introduced the engineering firm's team, including me. Mark stood and then announced that their group had also just signed a deal with the Montreal software company. They now owned that as well. Mark watched me closely. In fact, it felt like he never took his eyes off me. Within seconds, my breath was catching and my body was aching for him.

Falon, keep it professional!

After the introductions, we all sat down again and the reports by each person started. It was much like any meeting—boring. When it was my turn to get up and speak, I could feel the strength of Mark's gaze. It was as if he could see through my clothes and knew I was wearing a thong under my skirt—like he was undressing me, and his hands were wandering all over my skin right there in front of everyone. When I could feel desire start to choke me, I had to clear my throat a couple of times just so that I could continue. It's a good thing my presentation was only ten minutes, because any longer and I wouldn't have been able to keep standing.

When I took my seat again, I was tingling between my legs, and I could feel myself getting wet. This was just like that episode on the bus so many years ago, only much stronger. I concentrated on determining if it would show through for a second, and missed a question that had been directed at me.

"Ms Robertson?" Ray asked, "Could you please answer the question?"

"Oh, I'm sorry! I was lost in thought for a moment and didn't hear the question," I answered. I could feel my face turning bright red.

"Ms. Mitchell was asking you when your projection for the training component will be finished," said Ray.

"Ah, yes. Ms Mitchell, I should have that data for you within a week or so. We're still going through all the different tasks, and once I have them summarized and sorted according to job, then I'll be able to build a training program outline."

"'Thank you, Ms Robertson," said Gwen in the silkiest voice I had ever heard. I could feel the boys in the room start to melt. There would be puddles on their chairs in a few moments.

I glanced at Mark and saw that the effect he was having on me was the same effect that Gwen was having on the men in the room. Poor Ray, his tongue lolling out, panting like a puppy! At that moment, I distinctly felt a shiver go up my spine and the slightest of touches against my skin along the inside of my thigh, like I was naked. The sensation was sending me into places I'd rather not be in public!

"Ms Robertson," began Mark, "what do you foresee as the direction we should be taking with this project?"

He spoke so smoothly that I was watching his lips and listening to the sound of his voice rather than to the words he was speaking.

"Ah, well, um," I stammered, "I believe we should proceed according to the plan and see where that leads us," I answered.

What kind of an answer was that? I had lost control of my mind it seemed. All I wanted at that moment was to jump Mark's body, rip off his clothes, and sink his penis deep into me. Shaking myself back to reality, I looked at him and knew he was somehow making me think these things. I narrowed my eyes at him, warning him to behave himself—as if he could read my mind!

Then I felt something creeping up between my legs. When I rushed to stop it with my hand, I realized it was his foot. His toes were naked and reaching their destination. I felt his big toe touch me and I nearly gasped at the sensation. It took all my concentration to prevent myself from making a sound. His toe wiggled and started caressing my mound outside my thong. That was bad enough with my body reacting.

But when his toe found the edge of the thong and tucked inside, I had to cough to cover up the gasp that escaped my throat. His toe was working its way into the folds of skin and prying them apart. As his toes worked their way deeper into the cleft between my legs, the flush of heat that poured across my body left me having difficulty breathing.

I felt my legs try to separate in response, but my skirt was too tight. The only thing I could do was to sit there with my pad of paper on my lap and try not to react.

God, I hope my face isn't showing anything.

His toes were doing things to me that I didn't know they could do. Frankly, this was something I hadn't been prepared for. When I felt his big toe penetrate me, I thought I was going to die. I was having toe sex in the middle of a conference room with people around me, and I wanted to keep going! How were his legs that long? How could his toes do that? The sensations were driving me crazy.

I cast a quick glance around the table as others were talking. Luckily, no one seemed to be aware of what he was doing under the table, but Ray kept glancing at me every now and then.

Suddenly, it was over. He was pulling away; his foot was gone.

My senses came back to me and I saw that the conference was wrapping up and they were standing up. My head was starting to clear, but my knees felt too weak to support me at this moment. Ray was thanking everyone for coming to the meeting. I noticed he held Gwen's hand just a little too long, and looked into her eyes just a little too directly. Gwen pulled her hand from him and turned her shoulder to him as she walked over to Mark's side. Ray pouted then left. The others followed him out except for Gwen and Mark. I was still sitting down gathering up my things and putting them in my briefcase.

Gwen looked at me and smiled. I stood up and pushed my skirt down, which had risen up a notch or two, and held on to the table to steady myself.

"It's been a pleasure meeting you, Falon," she said, "Mark has told me a lot about you, and I see that it's all true. You really are a remarkable woman. Please marry him so that he doesn't wander around like a lost puppy anymore," she chided me gently. "We can't get any decent work out of him because he's constantly thinking of you!"

"Thank you, I think," I responded. Looking at Mark, I could see his eyes were dark pools again, deep with emotion and desire. It took all my focus to not cross the room at that moment.

"Falon," he started huskily, and had to clear his own throat, "I have another meeting with the owners of that restaurant this evening. Gwen is coming to meet them too, to see if we both agree about investing in them. Can I ask you to join us?"

"I don't see a reason why I should be there," I answered. "It's really between you and them, isn't it?"

"Yes, but I value your opinion very highly," answered Mark. "I genuinely would like your take on the presentation they have prepared for us tonight."

"Okay, when is the meeting?" I asked.

"At 7:00 tonight at your hotel," Gwen answered, "I've booked a conference room on the main floor."

"Okay, I'll be there," I answered.

They left the conference room together, but Mark cast one last look at me as he walked out the door. He licked his lips and blew me a kiss. I actually felt it land on my lips. I tentatively touched them before I finished packing up my things and leaving the conference room.

I needed to go to the bathroom to calm myself down and splash water on my face.

The rest of the afternoon was uneventful, except for the memory of those toes invading my panties. It was hard to concentrate.

After work I got back to the hotel by 6:30 and considered going to change before the meeting, but decided not to. Perhaps I could pay Mark back at this meeting. I asked Franco where the conference room was booked and was walking that way when I ran into Rick and his partner.

"Falon, aren't you a sight for sore eyes!" said Rick, hugging me, "You look absolutely irresistible tonight. Just look at the outfit!"

"Thanks, Rick. I'll be sitting in on your meeting with Mark Chisholm and Gwen Mitchell," I said.

"How do you know those people?" he asked me. Then I could see the memory come to his mind of Mark and I having dinner that night in his restaurant, "Oh yes, you two were at the restaurant last week, right?"

"Well, as it turns out, I'm a consultant on one of his other projects, and he wanted my opinion tonight. I guess I'll see you in there," I said as I continued down the hallway.

Entering the conference room, I could see that some people were already seated, so I took a seat in the back row on the aisle. This time, the room was laid out like a theatre with a podium at the front and all the chairs facing the same way in rows. Gwen was sitting in the first row near the centre aisle close to the presentation screen and away from me. Mark was sitting a row behind her. When I sat down, my skirt hiked up—perhaps a little farther than it would have normally. I covered my lap with my briefcase as I waited.

Once we were all seated, the lights went out and Rick and his partner took turns speaking at the front of the room. There were lots of charts, numbers, and slides. I wasn't really listening.

At the end of their presentation, Gwen asked Mark to present a little about their company, and to explain who they were and why they were interested in the restaurant.

Now I had an opportunity. While everyone else was facing forward except for Mark who was the only one facing me, I removed my briefcase from my lap. I watched as Mark noticed that he could see all the way up my skirt. Before the conference, I had removed my thong because it was damp and uncomfortable. I parted my legs a bit, (I knew that my skirt was higher!) and while he was looking, suggestively licked my lips with my tongue. I could see his reaction from the back of the room and I smiled. He went to stand behind the dais that was at the front then, but did not take his eyes away from me for long.

While he continued to speak, and I was not sure how because I was really pouring it on, everyone was watching him and the slides. I slid my hand between my legs and started to stimulate myself. Opening my legs farther so Mark could watch, I opened the lips of my clit to show him. Mark cleared his throat and stumbled on his words for a second. He looked away for a minute while he gathered his thoughts and continued. But it was only a moment or two until he looked again.

This time, while he kept up a running commentary about the slides on the screen, I slid my hand into my blouse and played with my breast. Then I undid the top button of my jacket and pulled my blouse over to one side enough so that the nipple popped out. Mark was almost transfixed for three seconds, and I could see a blush of heat around his neck.

Letting my breast go so that the nipple returned to its correct spot, I slid my hands down between my legs again. With two of the fingers on one hand, I started to masturbate. I had to concentrate on what he was saying to remain focused, but my delight in the desire I saw in his eyes made that possible.

I had no idea how he managed to finish the presentation, but when he started wrapping it up. I removed my hands, straightened up my clothes, and replaced my briefcase on my lap. When the lights came back on, I was the picture of propriety.

"Gwen, do you have anything to add?" he asked, after clearing his throat.

"No, Mark, I think you've just about covered everything you needed to," she answered with double-entendre. The smirk on her face showed she knew what was going on.

Mark had to put his portfolio in front of him as he walked back to a seat beside me this time.

"Thank you very much for that," he whispered into my ear. His voice was very thick with arousal.

Everyone stood and shook hands and said their goodbyes. Gwen and Mark indicated they would be in touch with the two chefs before the end of tomorrow. The chefs left the room with a great deal of hope.

Gwen then stood there and looked at Mark for a few long seconds.

"God, you look like you've just fucked for hours! Go get some sleep!" she said, then left the room.

Mark walked over and closed the conference room doors. We were alone again.

Coming over to me, he stood very close. He hiked up my skirt and his hand found its way to my clit in a flash. His not-so-gentle probing was a repeat of what I had done just a few minutes earlier, but of course it was so much better.

His other hand went behind my head while he kissed me deeply, his tongue mirroring the movements of his fingers. He very nearly brought me to climax right there, but stopped just before. His hand and his mouth withdrew all of a sudden, leaving me wanting him so much it almost hurt.

"I'll see you upstairs to finish this later," he said as he left the conference room.

I wasn't hungry for food at that moment, so I just went upstairs to wait for him. What else could I do? I was so horny now I could barely breathe!

While I was on my way up the elevator, my imagination kept my body experiencing the same sensations that Mark had driven me crazy with just a few moments ago. Once I was back in my room, I couldn't get out of my clothes fast enough. I was so hot and horny, I needed release. Lying on the bed, I pretended Mark was there and replayed the conference room scenario in my mind while my own fingers played the role of Mark. The orgasm rumbled over me releasing some of that energy.

Feeling centered and refreshed, I decided to change into something really sexy. Looking for my special lingerie, I changed into my red and black demi-bra that closed in the front, and the thong with the matching garter belt, and I had some nice stockings that would compliment the ensemble.

Once I was dressed, or undressed, really, I applied some Goddess Oil in some secret places. My body was still vibrating from the energy that had hit me from Mark, so I knew I had to calm down.

While I was waiting for him, I thought about the reality of who he was. He was immortal. We still had to talk that out—who and what he was, how I fit in. We'd had a close call with him biting me, but that turned out to not be a problem. So, this incredibly sexy man wanted me and he was immortal. He would live forever—well, much longer than me, and would never change appearance. What would it be like to grow old beside him? Could I?

More importantly, was I in love with him? That was the $64,000 question. I knew I had been in love with Zisis, and the confusion I felt over the Zisis/Mark thing was just that—confusion. My heart knew what to do. I needed to follow it and stop overthinking things. That was the one thing having sex with all these guys gave me: in spite of the variety, there really was only one man for me.

Apparently, my body knew what it wanted to do. I'd experienced lust, and sheer proximity to others hadn't done the same things to me. I could control myself around other handsome men. I couldn't control myself around Mark. It must be his pheromones. There was just something about him that pushed all my buttons the right way.

There were a lot of other big questions, but right now was not the time to address those.

Fifteen minutes later, there was a knock on my door announcing my meal was here. I grabbed a cover up and looked through the peephole. It was a bellhop, so I handed him a tip as I took my tray from him. I carried my grilled cheese sandwich and chicken noodle soup over to the couch to have my meal in front of the TV.

A little while later there was another knock on my door. I grabbed my silk robe again before I went to see if it was Mark. When I opened the door there was no one there. Looking up and down the hall there was no one to be seen. When I closed the door and turned around, Mark was sitting on the couch, watching me.

"How did you get past me?" I asked.

Mark grinned and came to me, wrapping his arms around me. I could smell hunger on him. It was the same scent he had earlier this evening in the conference room.

"Are you hungry?" I asked.

"Yes, for you," he answered.

16—Lora's Here!

Waking up with Mark again was nice. He was spooning me, and his arm was draped over my hip. I could feel his breathing on the back of my neck. It was a comforting position.

"Mark?" I whispered. "Are you awake?"

"Yes, I am. I was listening to your breathing."

"Is my breathing that interesting to listen to?"

"In fact, there are melodies that play out as you sleep."

I knocked him on the shoulder and smiled.

"I enjoyed last night. It was good to reconnect with you. But that doesn't mean everything is copesetic."

"I know, we have a lot to work out," he said. "But I feel we can."

"My best friend is coming down next weekend."

"Lora?" he asked.

"Yes. She should be here Thursday afternoon," I answered. "Will you be in town that weekend? Maybe we can make it a group thing."

"I will make that work."

Looking at the clock, it was 8:00 a.m., so I needed to get up and get to the office. The following week passed slowly, with regular life intruding on my plans for fun.

The day came for Lora to arrive, and I could barely concentrate. I told Ray I was leaving early to pick up my friend at the airport and was taking tomorrow off. He made some lewd comment about showing her around. Yeah, right.

Just before 4:00, Lora called to say that she had landed and was just waiting for customs and then her baggage. I told her I could pick her up because I had a rental car. Nothin fancy, but it got me back and forth from the hotel to the office. I told her I could immediately, and be at the airport within forty-five minutes. I was so excited that we would get to hang out this weekend!

Five o'clock saw me stuck in traffic only five minutes away from the airport. Lora was waiting outside the building on the sidewalk by the time I got there. I stopped the car and ran over to her. We hugged and screamed with happiness.

"Palm trees!" Lora squealed excitedly. "I didn't know there were palm trees here!"

"Yes, they're common in the South. Come on, I'll put your bags in the car. And we can get going. You pack a swimsuit?" I asked.

"No, I didn't think of it," replied Lora. "We have to go shopping!"

"Should that be our first stop?"

"Yes!" cheered Lora.

So we hit the mall on the way back to the hotel. Lora is more adventurous than I. When we found a swimsuit store, she found the tiniest suit possible that barely covered anything. Three triangles of fabric that covered nipples and crotch basically, all tied together with strings. Oh well, she could pull it off.

We got back to the hotel by 7:30 and dropped our packages in the room before going to dinner. Lora wanted to change for the evening, and I agreed. I set her in the second bedroom while I went to change in my room. The room phone rang.

"Hello," I answered.

"It's Mark, I'm downstairs."

"Okay, we'll be down in a minute, then we can go for dinner. How about the steakhouse again?"

"Sounds like a plan. I'll reserve a table and meet you there."

I decided on my black knit skirt and a black lacy top. The skirt was a clingy one, so I decided on no panties so that it wouldn't ride up while dancing. The lace top was a stretchy black camisole that was reasonably see-through. I wore a demi-cup black bra underneath that held my breasts up and together really nicely. Of course, because it was a demi-bra, the nipples almost peeked out from behind the lace.

Appraising myself in the mirror before I went out, I thought I was just too sexy looking. Lora came in at that moment and whistled.

"Wow, don't you look hot. Ouch!" she said, smiling widely. "What's got into you, Falon? You're not usually this racy!"

"I've been practicing, Lora. 'Sides, the guys down here are pretty cute, and the girls are gorgeous. I have to compete more openly."

"Well, girl, you've got it going on tonight. I like the nipples, barely hidden from view."

"Is it too much?" I asked, now a little self-conscious.

"Absolutely not!" she said. "Oh, by the way, don't wear panties, they make terrible lines in your skirt."

"I'm not."

"Neither am I!" she crowed. "Good times are coming!"

Lora was in a skin-tight, cream-coloured knit dress that was off the shoulder and gathered the whole length down the bodice. It was a very short dress, maybe an inch below her ass, but she had the legs to show off. She was wearing a wide black belt that had a big gold buckle, and black strappy four-inch heels to match. Lora had a large bust like me, and she was wearing a strapless push-up that made her look like a pinup star from the 1940s.

The guys won't know what hit them! One in white, one in black.

As we got off the elevator and crossed the lobby, people stopped and heads turned. For once it didn't feel like it was just for Lora. We left the hotel and walked the hundred steps to the steakhouse and entered.

Mark immediately saw me and stood up to indicate where he was. He'd reserved a table smack in the middle of the restaurant. Lora and I made our way over carefully.

"You two look stunning tonight!" gushed Mark.

"Hi, Mark, it's so nice to be going out on the town together again," said Lora.

"The team is back together!" I said.

At that moment, I saw Justin and Rick come out of the kitchen and make their way to our table. Rick stopped like a deer in headlights. He was staring at Lora like a starstruck fan.

Justin paused and grabbed him by the arm and pulled him forward.

"Good evening, Mr. Chisholm, Falon. Oh my, who is this vision? We haven't met, my name is Justin."

"Hi there, my name is Lora."

"She's my best friend and she's down for the weekend," I explained.

"This is my partner, Rick, we are the proprietors of this establishment and the chefs. Welcome, Lora."

I could see Lora sizing up these two men. One was gay, that was clear, but Rick didn't look gay, so she was confused by the title "partner." Lora had good gaydar.

"Thank you, Justin. Rick, you must come and sit with us later," she said, gambling he was straight.

"Um, certainly, when I'll bring the dessert for you," answered Rick. He sounded nervous.

As I watched Rick's reaction, I wondered if he was more than interested.

"I can take your orders, folks," said Rick.

"Excellent! I'll have the chef's choice," said Mark.

"Me too!" both Lora and I said together.

The chef's choice turned out to be succulent lobster with a Cobb salad and white pilaf rice. It was expertly done, and above all the dish looked beautiful. It was a shame to destroy the presentation just to eat it.

Our meal was relaxed as we all laughed at the stories going back and forth. It was good to be with my two favorite people in the world.

When dessert came, Rick personally brought it to our table as promised with four plates. Sitting beside Lora, he intended on staying.

"So, Lora, how long have you known Falon?" asked Rick.

"Oh, we go back a few years. We met through a mutual friend who is her neighbor and my babysitter," she answered.

"How did you get to know our Falon?" Lora asked him.

"We met at a mall about a month ago. When I learned she had a soft spot for the Tom Cats like me, I invited her to a concert at one of our bars. We've been friends since," said

Rick. "I must be forward and say, Lora, you are a truly beautiful woman. May I take you dancing later tonight?"

"Oh, Rick, I'd love that." Lora winked at me.

"Rick, we were planning things for this weekend. Would you be able to make it a foursome?" I asked.

"Unfortunately, I am going to Miami this weekend."

"Oh! What for?"

"Restaurant business. Justin and I have to be there."

"Are you and Justin a couple?" asked Lora.

Rick looked blankly at her for a moment. "No, not at all, just business partners. Is that what ... oh, gee, sorry. No, we're not a couple. I'm very much into women," He smiled an electric smile and all that Latin charm poured out. I think I saw Lora melt a little. I knew she had a soft spot for Latin men.

"Then why don't we accompany you?" Lora boldly asked. "After all, it's more fun as a group."

I looked at Mark and he caught my drift.

"That's a splendid idea, Lora. We could drive down in two cars and make a weekend of it. Miami is so much better than Atlanta."

17—Planning a Road Trip

The four of us sat around the table and brainstormed about the weekend. We agreed to leave Friday morning and drive to Miami. Mark was going to book a hotel for us for Friday and Saturday. Saturday was the award dinner so that was taken care of. What would we do on Friday?

"The Tom Cats are playing in Miami on Friday," said Mark. "I can get us four tickets."

"Oh, great idea," I said. "How long a drive is it to Miami?"

"About nine and a half hours. So we should leave early."

"Rick, what do we need to wear?"

"For the Awards? It's a black-tie affair. So gowns?" Did you bring anything like that?" he asked.

"Nope, I surely didn't," said Lora. "I guess I'll have to go shopping."

"Never you mind, I'll take care of it for you," said Rick. Lora and I looked at each other and shrugged.

"I tell you what, you kids go and dance, I'm going to bed. Mark, are you coming?" I asked pointedly.

"Don't have to ask me twice. Let me go pay the bill."

"Oh, no need. You've been comped for the evening. Justin's word," said Rick. "And I will take you up on stealing this goddess to go and dance."

"See you tomorrow morning around 8:00 for breakfast?" I asked.

"Yes, hon, don't wait up for me," said Lora as she gazed at Rick.

"Well, I think they'll hit it off, don't you?" I asked Mark once we were on the elevator. "In the meantime, are you staying?"

"I'd like to, if I may."

"Please. Want to join me in the shower?"

"Hmmm, that is an offer I cannot refuse," he said, starting to pull his clothes off as soon as we walked into the room.

By the time he was naked, he was already showing his arousal. He followed me to the bathroom and I got back under the water. He gazed at me a moment or two, the water sluicing over my head and running down in rivulets between my breasts and dripping off my nipples. He stepped into the shower then and took one of my breasts in between his lips and gently sucked on it, licking the water droplets from its tip.

He took me into his arms, holding me against his body again. I could feel an energy coming through his skin; it felt like gentle pins and needles on my nipples, stomach, and hips.

We stood there for maybe five or six minutes, letting the hot water pour over our heads, locked in an embrace. I felt his energy and his erection getting stronger and stronger. I pulled away from him to look up to his face. His eyes were closed, and there was a smile on his lips. He opened his eyes when he felt me move. He gazed down at me.

"I am so happy when I'm with you," he stated simply.

"Do you want to be happier?" I flirted.

"Always."

I took possession of his erection and started massaging its length. I kneaded my fingertips along him, grasping his scrotum and gently squeezing. Rubbing him was a little like rubbing a magical lamp—a genie always came out. I giggled at my thought.

He looked at me questioningly, but I didn't answer him. Instead, I knelt down in the shower and started kissing his head, licking the water droplets off the tip of his penis. He quivered in my touch and his erection grew as if it were reaching out to touch me.

Again, I wrapped my lips around the sensitive, swollen tip. It was quite a mouthful! I still don't know how girls take an entire guy into their mouths!

Mimicking his action inside me, I moved my tongue up and down, and tried to draw him into my mouth as far as I could go without gagging. He was watching me from above, and let out a deep quiet moan.

"I can't stand this anymore," he groaned, and lifted me to stand before him again. "Gorgeous woman, let me love you. I need you so much, Falon. Ah God, ohhhh," he groaned loudly this time.

I stood up and pulled his cock between my legs, watching him when he said that. My heart melted. I felt the same way. I guided him into me. There was a big difference in our heights though, and we laughed when we just couldn't make it work standing. He picked me up to his waist level and I wrapped my legs around his hips. This perfectly aligned his shaft with my vagina, and he plunged into me. Grabbing towels, he carried me out of the shower and into the bedroom. He separated from me just long enough to lay me on the floor on the towels. The separation of his body from mine was short, but the empty ache I felt was acute.

When he got down on the floor too, he hovered over me as if in a push-up position. We weren't touching, except that his penis was reaching for me. I opened my legs and wrapped them around his hips, opening myself for him to take me.

As always, the moment of his penetration was exquisite. He fit so perfectly and filled me so much it made me orgasm each time. He held his place, allowing the orgasm to dissipate and my body to return to him. He pulled out, and with a gasp pushed in slowly, inching his way inside me so that I could feel his length as it was absorbed by my body.

It wasn't only his length that was oversized, he was thick too. I couldn't get my hand all the way around his shaft so that my finger and thumb met. It took two hands to hold him all the way around. So the pressure against the walls of my vagina was hard.

When he had reached the end of my vagina, I could feel him pressing on the inside lips of my womb with his penis. The sensation hurt a little, but not a pain that was intense.

"Ah—ah," I cried out.

He almost pulled out at that point. Only my legs locked around his hips prevented that. He looked down at me and I could see concern in his eyes.

"It's okay," I reassured him. "Slow hurts a little, that's all."

"Painful? I didn't know I caused you pain. I should stop!"

"Don't you dare!" I flashed anger.

"Would you have me cause you pain?"

"It's not that kind of pain," I explained. "I want you inside me, completely, so thrust hard!"

He took my direction, and with one thrust he pushed his length to the very end. He gasped then too with the sensation of tipping me. I could feel how that excited him even more; his erection became more pronounced for a moment. I sensed that he was close to losing control.

Once he was ready, he started pulling and pushing himself in and out of me, the rhythm of a rumba dance, slow and sensual. Each time, he completely filled me so that he tipped the end of my vagina. It made me shudder, and sent ripples moving outward through both of our bodies.

Yet we were not building to a climax. We were in this state of high arousal, especially him, without any loss of control. It was like being high on tequila—you could see and hear everything better in some ways, yet it was all distorted and distant somehow.

He was on his knees now, still inside me, but with his legs in between mine, and he was lifting my ass with his hands with my legs on either side of him bent to the floor past his hips. I couldn't do much, but he was able to drive so hard into me it left me gasping and moaning and breathless. His body was close to mine; it was very intimate, more so than other positions. He was able to completely take me this way.

His slow thrusts were erotic and sensual. He was taking his time and bringing me along with him. The deep thrusting was starting to make him lose it though. I could see his face and how he strained to keep his release contained. I took his face in my hands and brought it down between my breasts and squeezed them together to give him lots of cleavage. He sucked and nipped and licked at them while he was trying to thrust into me. It was too much for him to manage.

"Falon, I'm losing it," he groaned.

"Let it go," I whispered.

He started unraveling and my ride started. The rhythm changed and the thrusts got faster as he built toward orgasm, his scrotum banging into me with each push.

I was starting to climax now; he could see that. He let go of control and hammered me hard. The enormous head of excitement that had built up exploded and took both of us as we reached orgasm together. He emptied his seed deep inside my womb, and a fantasy crossed my mind that this time would bear fruit.

I could feel his head quivering inside me as he bent to my neck, licked the spot where it joined my shoulder and bit down.

It completely spent him. Both our bodies shuddered with the shared release as his venom flowed into me and sent me into the stratosphere.

It took a while to come down. When I did, I found him leaning forward with his head on my breasts and he was smiling and breathing hard.

"Oh God, you are wonderful! I love you so much," he whispered.

I couldn't speak yet, so I grunted.

"Falon, my beautiful woman, you are something else," he breathed into the space between my breasts. "I cannot believe how completely I can be myself with you. I have never been able to before. I am totally addicted to you."

"You make me feel so sexy and wanted," I murmured.

"Can you stand?" he asked.

"Do I have to? I guess we're about to find out, no?"

"I don't want to come out," he said, "but we need to get to bed. My knees hurt!"

Chuckling, he slowly pulled himself out of me. He was still semi erect, still long. It seemed he was never quite finished. It felt like he was removing a pole from me. When his head was finally at the very edge, he held there a minute with the tip gently pushing against me. Then he moved away and a torrent of semen followed him. Maybe this time we'd created a life—it was certainly the most powerful sex I had ever had.

Eventually, he stood up and retrieved a towel and hot cloth from the bathroom and washed me down carefully. He caressed me with the soapy water and gently dried my skin with loving strokes. He helped me to stand; my knees were weak—the sex was that good. He carried me to the bed and we just lay there in each other's arms.

We must have fallen asleep or dozed, because the phone startled me awake. I rolled over and picked up the phone.

"Hello?" I answered the phone.

"Hey, girlfriend, it's me!" said Lora.

"Hey what's up?" I asked her.

"Well, I'm here at Rick's place. I'm going to stay the night," she said. "Is Mark there now?" Lora asked.

"Hmmm, yup," I answered.

"You just had fucking good sex, didn't you?" she asked.

"Hmmm, yup," I answered with a giggle.

"Bitch!" she giggled too. "I'm hoping for me too. Rick is gorgeous!"

"Yes, he's very cute. He's good with his hands too—he's a baker. He's actually kind of shy and very nice. You'll have fun."

"Is he good in bed?" asked Lora, cutting to the chase.

"I think he will be—he certainly knows his way around lady parts!" I answered.

Mark opened his eyes just then and looked at me with an unspoken question on his lips.

"It's Lora," I told him.

"I heard that," he answered me. "You have not had sex with Ricardo?" he asked me.

"Nope."

"Is Mark talking to you, dear?" Lora asked me. "Does he want to fuck you again? Should I let you go to finish him off?"

"Yes, no, and no," I said. "Besides, I don't think I can finish him off. So should we make it a foursome?"

"You can't finish him off? He's always hard? Oh my yes!" she said. "It'll guarantee me some sex this weekend."

Always the pragmatist, my friend Lora!

"I think Rick and I will be picking you up and driving straight there."

"Sounds like a plan. See you tomorrow morning," I answered.

I replaced the phone and rolled back to Mark.

"So what's the verdict?" he asked me.

"Yes, they will pick us up here tomorrow morning," I responded.

"Did I hear you talking about a Miata MX-5 with Lora? What's that about?"

"Rick has a brand new one. They just came out and I'm lusting after that car! I want one so bad it's stupid! They're so sexy and gorgeous and they look like loads of fun to drive."

"I'll see what I can do then."

"What do you mean? You don't drive one. I was going to call the rental company to see if they have them available to rent. I would trade in the 626 I'm driving now for the MX-5 on the weekend."

"Oh I see," he said. He had a thoughtful look on his face, like he was thinking of doing something and was trying to figure out how.

Mark was distracting me by drawing circles on my skin around my nipples and around my breasts. It was making it difficult to think straight. It was hard to believe that after that intensely satisfying lovemaking, he was arousing me yet again.

His answer was to roll on his back, bring me on top of him and continue his caressing. This time, he grabbed my ass and pulled me down against his shaft. I rubbed myself on him until I could feel him jump between us. I lifted my body up enough so that I could free him from my trap. I guided him inside me again, and slid my body down over him like a glove. I sat up then, straddling him, my full weight resting on his hips. He was looking up at me: those gold rings were starting to swirl around his irises again.

We made love again, me on top in one of my favorite positions. When we were done, I stayed straddling him for a few minutes to let my heart rate slow down and my breathing return to normal. I sat with my eyes closed just relishing in the sensation of him being deep inside me. There was no pain in this position whatsoever. I could feel him inside wiggling now, telling me he was still semi-rigid.

He could feel it too.

"You know, you have a remarkable set of pipes," he said. "I know that I am significantly larger than average men, and yet you can take all of me. I can feel when I reach that inner sanctum of yours and it feels amazing."

"Mmmm, yes, I agree."

"How did I get so lucky?" he asked.

"Hmmm," I murmured. I lay down on his chest; my head reached to almost the small depression in his neck. I could place my ear on his breast and listen to his heartbeat. It was reassuringly strong and steady. I started dozing off like that, with him inside, and his arms around me.

There was a knock on the door, and a bellhop announced our food had arrived.

"Please leave it outside, I'll come and get it," yelled Mark. "I have no intention of pulling out right now."

"Mmmm," I said. "But the food will get cold."

"So what?" he said.

"I hate cold eggs," I complained.

"Okay," he replied, pulling out.

A small whine escaped me as he slid out and I was suddenly empty again. The semen was dribbling out. Mark grabbed a towel from the bathroom for me before answering the door. I could hear murmured voices as he tipped the bellhop. He brought the trolley into the living room.

However, I was so content that I fell into a blissful sleep.

18—Miami

Friday morning broke beautifully. I was so excited about the weekend I was up before dawn. I opened up the glass doors to watch the sunrise from the hotel room. I had already packed the night before, so I was ready to leave. I had my shower and was dressed too. I had finally got the knack of making coffee in that silly little hotel room coffee maker, and purchased myself a carton of real coffee cream and sugar. It wasn't great, but it was better than nothing.

Mark was still in bed. It was debatable whether he was asleep though. He didn't seem to need sleep that much. Every time I woke up last night, he was wide awake already and watching me.

I was standing in front of the living room window watching the sun come up. I had opened the window earlier to feel the morning air. Mark came into the room and stood behind me, wrapping his arms around my waist.

When the first rays of the sun hit us, he stood in the sunshine and sighed just like me. The warmth of the rays was nice. After a minute, he released me and went to get some coffee. I turned around and followed him with my eyes.

"Hey, Mark, did you bring enough clothes with you?" I asked him.

"Yes, I think so," he answered.

"You remembered a swimsuit?"

"Do I have to wear one?" he teased me.

"Only on public beaches," I answered. "By the way, where are we staying?"

"I've booked us two suites at the St. Regis Bal Harbor. They're king suites and have two beds."

"That sounds expensive," I noted.

"Ah, about $3300 a night," he answered.

"Is that $3300 dollars a night, per person?" I choked out.

"Yes. It's a nice hotel with very good service and a private nude beach. We own it," he added.

"Oh, you own the hotel? So you don't have to pay for it?"

"Oh yes, we don't get freebies, just discounts."

I had never stayed in a hotel room that cost that much. *It'd better be pretty spectacular.*

Promptly at 8:30, there was a knock on my door. Mark went to answer it, and it was Rick.

"Good morning, Ricardo," Mark greeted him.

"Good morning, but please call me Rick!" he replied. "If we're going to be hanging out together with these two beautiful women, we might as well be friends!"

"Sounds good," said Mark guardedly. "Where's Lora?" He was looking Rick up and down, not sure if he trusted him.

"She's on her way up," he answered. "She stopped at the restaurant for some reason."

"Oh, Mark, don't be so protective!" I chided him. Mark threw me a look that made me weak in the knees.

"Shall we wait for her?" I asked both of them. "Oh, Mark, I couldn't get the Miata for the weekend. So we'll just have to take the 626."

"It's okay, Falon, I have a surprise for you," he said.

Another knock happened and the door opened on its own. Lora came running in the room squealing in delight.

"It's nice to be back here," said Lora. "Falon, where are you?"

"In the bedroom getting the suitcases," I called out. "This is going to be so much fun!"

"Indeed," said Lora as she took Rick's arm and they led the way out.

We grabbed our bags and headed down to the lobby. Mark and Rick asked the valet to bring their cars to the front. We stood there waiting while two valets went to get them.

The next thing I see is a cherry red MX-5 driving up to the front door, with another—jet black—behind it.

"Whose black Miata is that?" I asked.

"It's Justin's," said Rick. "We purchased the same car. He's loaning me this one because he wanted the red one for the event at the restaurant tomorrow. Don't tell me why it had to be red, but we switched cars this weekend."

"Then whose is the red one?" I asked.

"That one's yours," answered Mark.

"Mine? I don't have a Miata," I answered.

"Now you do. It's your birthday gift. I didn't have a chance to get you something you really wanted, so when I found out about the MX-5, I had one ordered on Tuesday morning. She's brand-new. Fifteen miles on her, so you have to break her in a bit before you let yourself go crazy, okay?"

"Mine?"

"Yours."

I turned around and was about to say, "You shouldn't have," when Mark put a finger on my lips to shush me.

"Yes, I did have to. It's a small thing really for one I care so deeply about," he said quietly.

Then he handed me the key and we walked over to see the car. She was beautiful! Cream coloured leather seats and a convertible!

"It's such a beautiful car, but don't they usually have black interiors?" I asked.

"Yes, they do, but I special ordered this one to have a cream-coloured interior. Trust me on this one, with the convertible you want light coloured seats!" Mark replied.

"Well, what are we waiting for?" asked Rick. "Let's go!"

We jumped in the cars and took off. I was finally driving my dream car!

Wow! Mark had taken the precaution of getting a complete set of road maps so that we could navigate and hopefully not get lost! I'd never driven to Florida, so the maps were handy to have.

For the first part of the trip, Mark agreed to let Lora sit with me so we could talk, and he and Rick traveled together.

By the time we had crossed the state line, Mark and Rick seemed to have a friendship sprouting. Rick and I were having fun racing each other in between rest stops. We changed seating just past Lake City, Florida. Lora went to be with Rick, and Mark came to be with me.

"Do you want to drive?" I asked Mark.

"Sure, if you would let me. I like this little car. Maybe I'll get one for myself. They're very inexpensive for what you get," he replied.

So I handed him my key and he got behind the wheel. Of course, being a sports car it was a small cockpit. I was only 5'4" tall, so it was a perfect fit for me. Mark, on the other hand, stood 6'3" tall, so it was a bit of a squeeze for him. But he fit.

Thankfully, the seat was completely adjustable so that he could make himself reasonably comfortable.

We took off again after the lunch stop in Lake City, and the interstate turned into Florida's turnpike and a toll road. That took us past Disney World and Orlando and continued on south, making for the eastern coastline.

By the time we reached Fort Pierce, we were within smelling distance of the ocean. And by the time we got as far as Palm Beach, we could see the ocean every now and then from the highway. I suggested that we get off the turnpike and use the coastline highway A1A so we could skirt the coast and see the ocean. I got voted down though because everyone wanted to get there quickly.

We reached Miami by 5:30—just in time for dinner! We looked for the hotel Mark had booked on the beach and checked in first.

The room was luxurious and well appointed. Each suite had a king and a queen in separate rooms, with a dining and living area too.

Mark gave a set of keys to Lora and Rick and they went to their suite. They were having fun together. Since I hadn't seen them together yet, it was nice to see them get along so well. We told the guys we'd meet them downstairs 'cause we wanted to change into fresh clothes for dinner. Lora was wearing a slinky silver clingy dress that had a cowl neckline and no back. It was very short, of course, and she completed her drop-dead look with very high stiletto shoes.

I had put on a little black dress that had wide crossed straps in the back attached to a skirt that started at my hips. The front was a cross-over low-cut neckline, and the waist was cinched tight. I was also wearing heels, because as short girls we had the advantage of having tall guys to escort us.

When the two of us walked out of the elevator, the boys had drop-dead expressions on their faces. I walked over to

Mark and picked up his jaw for him and Lora took Rick's hand and turned him around toward the car. I think we were a hit.

The guys for their part were well turned out too. Mark always looked good, but he was looking very urban-chic tonight. Rick was very elegant looking as well.

We found a seafood restaurant and had dinner, then went walking down the street looking for entertainment. There were lots of clubs in Miami, so it didn't take long to find something that looked like fun.

It was nice having two very-well dressed men with us, because the meat market in Miami was voracious. If Lora and I had been alone, we might not have made it out of here intact. The men were quite aggressive. As we were walking toward a table, one guy tried to grab Lora and slip his hand inside her dress. Rick was quick to react and made sure the guy understood that Lora was off limits. I didn't need to worry; Mark just had to look at a jerk and then he backed off.

We danced until 1:30 or 2:00 a.m., then left the club in favor of a walk on the beach. That's another thing we wouldn't have done if we hadn't had the guys with us. The beach can be kind of scary at night. But it was romantic when it was just the four of us. Lora and I took our shoes off and encouraged the boys to do the same. Soon we were all walking in the sand in our bare feet. Mark rolled his pants up and walked into the waves far enough for the surf to wash over his toes. He was standing there mesmerized by the rhythm of the waves and the feeling of the warm water on his feet.

"It's nice here, isn't it?" I asked him.

"Very," he answered. "I'm very glad it's the four of us, though. I'd hate to think of you girls handling those aggressive men by yourselves."

"Yeah, that was a bit creepy. I'm glad you're here too," I said, snuggling under his arm.

"So it seems Rick likes Lora a lot, and the feeling looks reciprocated," Mark asked.

"Yeah, it does look that way. I'm glad, because Lora needs a good guy for a change," I answered.

I looked down the beach to where they were walking arm-in-arm, weaving along the sand. Lora was laughing hysterically, and I could hear Rick's low chuckle as well. They seemed to be getting along fine.

"Hey, guys, wait up!" I called out to them.

They turned around and stopped walking. I could see them discussing something, and then Rick turned to Lora and embraced her and gave her a kiss. Lora was returning the kiss, so that was a good sign.

Slowly, they made their way back to us and stood in the waves with us.

"Should we get these ladies home?" Rick asked Mark.

"I think it's time we get them to bed, yes," agreed Mark.

Lora and I giggled as we ran, hand in hand, away from the boys across the sand.

"Of course, we'll have to catch them," chuckled Rick.

"That's half the fun!" said Mark.

When we got back to our rooms, it was pretty easy to split. Rick led Lora to one room and we went to the other. Shortly after all the lights were out, I could hear murmurs from Lora and Rick's room, followed by more vigorous activity. That would be something we girls would compare when the boys weren't around. Mark and I also made love, but we did it quietly. At least I think so.

The following morning, I woke up early, just too excited to stay in bed. I rolled over to see if Mark was asleep, and he wasn't. He was lying there with his eyes wide open.

"Good, you're awake! Let's get up. Early mornings on the beach are always really nice."

"I'll grab my sunglasses!" he agreed.

After putting on swimsuits and grabbing towels, we quietly left the room and went down to the beach. The sun had just started rising over the ocean. The colors of the morning were spectacular: pinks and reds criss-crossed the sky painted on clouds.

"Hey, doesn't that rhyme go 'red sky at night, sailor's delight, red sky in the morning, sailor take warning?'" Mark asked.

"Yeah, I think so. That means there might be a storm or something. But right now the sky is clear, so let's go collect shells and stake out a spot to sit."

We walked a little way from the entrance of the hotel on the beach and found a nice flat spot to set up our towels and chairs. The hotel also had sunshades that you could rent by the day, so we did that in case anyone else needed to stay under cover from the sun. Mark was delighted that he could sit out here with me and still be in the shade.

An hour or so later, we saw Lora and Rick coming down the beach carrying their towels and chairs too. When they got to us, Lora immediately laid out her towel beside me and sat down.

"Rick, could you please oil me?" Lora asked.

"Sure."

Lora dropped her cover up to display the itsy-bitsy bikini that barely covered anything and again Rick's jaw went slack. He might never recover from Lora, but at least he was a nice guy. Lora handed him her suntan oil and he started liberally applying it to her back because she was lying on her stomach first. When Lora undid the ties holding her top on, I think Rick almost lost it, but he kept going. *What a trooper!*

I glanced at Mark and noticed he was smiling with amusement under the sunshade. He'd been out with Lora and I before, so he had a better understanding of what was going to happen today.

"Falon, do you need any suntan oil too?" asked Mark.

"Sure, my back would be great. Thanks," I answered.

Mark took his time applying the oil everywhere. I was wearing my now famous zippered one piece, so there was less skin to burn on my body.

The guys sat under the shade and were talking and reading while us ladies were bronzing our bodies in the sunshine. We were there for about two hours, when I noticed I was hungry because we hadn't had breakfast yet.

"Hey, Lora, you hungry?" I asked her.

"Yeah, a little. Didn't have food this morning. Did you?"

"No, we came out here early to watch the sunrise."

"Are you girls hungry? Can we get you something to eat?" asked Mark.

"Yes please!" we said in unison. The guys laughed.

"Anything specific?" Rick asked.

"Eggs, toast, bacon, coffee, that would be nice," suggested Lora.

"Coming right up," answered Mark. "You too, Falon? Same thing?"

"That would be great! Thanks, Mark."

So the guys left us there and went in search of food for all of us. I expected they would be gone for an hour or so, which gave Lora and I time to compare notes!

"So did you have fun last night?" I started.

"He's great! What a find! Excellent in bed too. How did you meet him again?" asked Lora. I told her the story of how we met in the shopping center.

"I really like this one, Falon. He's a real sweetheart," said Lora. "We have hit it off too. He's got a quirky sense of humor like me, and is interested in my life. What a sweet change. Of course, he's my type. You know I can't resist a Latino. Oh my God, he's gorgeous. And it helps that the sex was pretty spectacular. He is very nicely hung, thank you very much."

"I'm glad, because if you two hadn't hit it off, it would have been a difficult weekend."

"Ah you know me, I make pie out of sour apples. Besides, as long as he's decent I can have a good time. This one's decent, sexy, good-looking, rich, and talented!" she said. "I could love a guy like this," she sighed wistfully.

"Really? Lora O'Reilly could fall in love?" I teased her.

"Shhhh," she stopped me. "I never tell. But he hits me just right in all the best places."

We stopped talking for a few minutes. Lora sat up to adjust her bathing suit. Of course, when she sat up, it came off completely, and for a moment or two she was sitting topless on the beach in Miami. The beach wasn't empty either. But this was a private beach and nudity was allowed. There were a few couples who were nude.

So she shed the rest of her suit and laid out front up. Some people noticed, but most didn't. The ones who did watched with interest at what we were doing. The guys' tongues were lolling out, and I could swear some of them were saluting right there. But no one did anything or made a scene.

Lora got out the oil and slathered on her front while we had an audience. We were looking around the beach playing the same game we did at the Peel Pub. We started discussing the people, picking out the losers and winners. Here it seemed there were two kinds of people too: natives and tourists. It was pretty easy to tell who was which too. The tourists were pale or red, and the natives were deep brown.

There were a lot of single guys here too—some sitting in pairs and others in groups. No one was alone. That was interesting. There were lots of single women too. There the similarity ended. Most of the single women were alone. There were a couple of groups, but mostly the women were individuals.

The guys were watching the women of course, but the women were watching each other too. A few were keeping their eye on us now that the men had left. I guess we might be looked at as competition. There's another reason I was glad we're a foursome this weekend.

One particular woman was obviously on the hunt. She was a tall, leggy blonde; attractive, but not pretty. She had the look of a woman who would not retain her looks past thirty. She was not really a standout in any way, yet there was always a guy talking to her. There was a steady stream of guys walking up to her and talking to her. She seemed to turn them away for the most part.

Until a pair of guys came out onto the beach. One was obviously of Italian descent; the other I couldn't tell, but he had strawberry blond hair. He was a nice-looking man but he looked sad. The Italian looked like he thought the world of himself and strutted across the beach like he was surveying his harem.

When they settled on a spot, not too far from where we were sitting, we could overhear some of their conversation. The Italian was trying to get the other one to cheer up and had brought him to Miami to forget some girl. The Italian was pointing out girls on the beach to his friend and they were discussing their attributes. No, that one was too small, or too young, or too brown, or not a blonde, or not shapely enough. Wow, were they shopping?

Lora and I eavesdropped a little just to see if we could figure out who they would zoom in on. We didn't have to wait too long because the leggy blonde decided to take matters into her own hands.

She got up off her towel, adjusted her breasts so they were almost coming out of her bikini, and walked with an exaggerated sway past the two guys toward the drink cabana on the beach. The Italian didn't notice, but the red-haired guy's eyes popped out of his head. Bull's eye! He watched her walk to get a drink and then back to her towel where she carefully, skilfully, arranged her body to its best viewing advantage from their point of view. Her legs were opened toward them, and the drink was positioned between her legs on the towel.

Really? Please! How obvious can you get! When she bent over to put lotion on her feet, she gave a very good opportunity to anyone who wanted one to see her entire chest for it came out of her suit completely. She was actually kinda small—compared to Lora and me, that is.

Lora and I watched this tableau for a while, but nothing seemed to happen, so we lost interest and started watching other people on the beach.

Finally Mark and Rick returned with food.

"Ah, hello ladies!" came the call from Mark.

He came up on my side and hadn't noticed Lora was nude yet.

I pointed out Ms. Legs. Mark looked at her for a few seconds before turning back to me and shaking his head.

"That one's a gold-digger. I've seen them all over, and they have the same tactics wherever they go—trouble with a capital T," he said.

Rick walked around Lora's side.

"Ah, Lora, you are truly a beautiful woman. I'm going to have trouble keeping my hands off of you," he said quietly to her as he knelt down.

"You say the nicest things," Lora whispered back to him. She wasn't putting on anything either, no accent, no bawdiness. I think she really liked him.

"Who?" Rick said. "Oh that one, yeah, trouble. Only a guy with a broken heart or a fool will be taken in by the likes of her. Of course, she'll separate him from his bankroll fast enough. It was a woman like that who turned me off relationships completely for a while. I just wasn't interested—especially if they were all like that!"

"I hear you," remarked Mark. "Women like that give the good ones a bad name. I too almost fell victim to one of those harlots."

"Really?" I asked.

"Yeah, in my early twenties, I met a long-legged blonde, just like her. She cost me a lot of money for the grief she gave me."

"So who's her target?" asked Rick.

"That nice-looking guy over there with the Italian. The Italian thinks he's God's gift to women, but the friend seems sad. We heard them talking about getting over a girl."

"Poor guy, this is the last place you should be if your heart is broken," said Rick.

"Definitely right there, my friend," agreed Mark.

"So what did you get us?" asked Lora.

"What you asked for, and more," said Rick with a flourish.

The two of them walked behind the sunshade and returned with trays of food.

"Mark knows the head chef at this hotel, which is good, because the kitchen wasn't making breakfast anymore. He pulled some strings and they whipped us up some breakfast," said Rick.

"We've got croissants, bacon, French Toast, coffee, fruit, and eggs," continued Mark.

"Amazing!" cried Lora. "How did you manage that?"

"How do you guys keep doing this for us? Making all these connections and spoiling us so much. Careful, or we could get used to this."

"Really? How marvelous," Lora cried. "And ya, I'm getting real used to being treated like a queen. How am I ever going to go home?"

Breakfast on the beach was a hit. We had people coming up to us to ask where we had found the food. Each time the story grew more elaborate, and we were hooting at the exaggerations of the boys with each telling.

We spent the rest of the day in peaceful bliss playing in the waves, sitting on the beach, taking long walks. Whenever Lora and I went in the water, the guys followed closely. Neither of them wanted us to be attacked by the two-footed sharks patrolling the beach that day.

Around five o'clock we called it a day and went in to dress for dinner.

"Mark, we didn't bring anything with us, remember? I don't have a gown and neither does Lora," I said.

"Ah, don't worry about that. You girls go to our room. You'll find a surprise there," said Mark.

"Mark and I will get dressed in our room," said Rick.

We all went up stairs and split off to get dressed. Hanging in our room Lora and I found two garment racks filled with gowns all in our sizes. We got to choose what we wanted. Plus there was matching jewelry and shoes.

"Wow, how did they do this?" asked Lora.

"I have no idea," I said. "But just look at these dresses. What do you want to wear?"

Lora chose a black gown that had a slit from the neck to almost the top of her groin going diagonally from the left breast across her abdomen and down her right leg. The slit had little loops across it fastened with rhinestone buttons. The buttons ended at the top of her leg, leaving the rest of the slit open. It too had a very deep neckline in the back. She couldn't wear a bra or panties either because they would show too. Like me, she worked with a silicone bra that held up the girls but allowed for a natural shape.

I chose a fire red gown that gathered the entire length of the dress and was very tight. There was no room for panties under this number. There was a slit up the back of the dress right to the crack in my ass, and the front was scooped down below my waist with a cowl. I had to use body tape to keep it from exposing my boobs. It draped over my shoulders loosely. I wore one of those stick-on silicone bras that pushed up your boobs—not that I needed a push up, but I needed something with D cups—so my breasts were perky all night.

There's something stimulating about the fabric of your dress constantly brushing your nipples. *It's a good thing my bust hasn't drooped yet!*

There was a beautiful diamond pendant for me to wear and a pair of earrings to match. Lora had styled my hair so that it flowed down my back in big bouncy curls.

Lora picked out a ruby necklace that was like fire, with matching drop earrings. I did her hair and swept it up into an elegant chignon at the back and pinned it in place with diamond and ruby studded pins and clips.

When the guys came over to the room to pick us up, I thought they were going to have heart attacks.

"Oh my God, you two are stunning, like movie stars," said Rick.

"We'll be fighting off suitors all night," Mark agreed.

"No, we won't," said Rick. "I'll be keeping this one very close," he said as he gathered up Lora in his arms.

"Well, you two are pretty gorgeous too. You cleaned up nicely!" I teased them.

Rick was truly gorgeous in a deep-burgundy tuxedo with a paler coloured shirt in the same hue. It was very striking. Mark looked as elegant as could be in a traditional tuxedo and a white shirt.

"Oh boy, Mark, I think we're in trouble tonight," said Rick, watching us walk down the hallway to the elevator.

"Rick, you may be right, my man. But this is the kind of trouble I dream of," said Mark.

"Indeed," was the response. "How'd we get so lucky?"

"I don't really know, but I'm not asking questions of the Fates tonight. I'm the luckiest man in the world right now," whispered Mark.

"My thinking too," replied Rick.

"So, Rick, where are we going?" asked Lora. She had a secret little smile on her face.

"You'll see when we get there," he answered cryptically.

"Do you know?" I asked Mark.

"Nope," he answered. "Rick's keeping that answer close to the vest."

Our cars were waiting for us at the front door of the hotel. The boys helped us into our seats like true Southern gentlemen. That was a good thing, because my dress would have given all the surrounding folks a real show! As we got in the car, I overheard comments from the people walking by like "the women outshone even those beautiful cars" and "the women were wearing the same colors as the cars." I hadn't noticed that!

Mark and Rick drove so that we could just sit there and look gorgeous. Mark had to follow, because Rick wouldn't tell us where we were going.

Half an hour later, we pulled up in front of a really fancy hotel. There was a red carpet laid out from the front door, and there were all kinds of photographers there taking pictures of the people walking in. Everyone entering was formally dressed. It looked like the Oscars everyone was so fancy.

Rick drove right to the front door and a doorman rushed to open the doors of our cars and helped Lora and I out. The guys walked around the cars and offered their arms to us and we stepped along the red carpet to get inside. The cameras were flashing and I felt like a movie star.

It was a little strange, walking a red carpet like that. As soon as we were inside the hotel, Rick walked us up to the main desk and introduced himself.

"Oh, Mr. Benal, it's nice that you could make it after all. You have a party of four with you?" asked the gentleman behind the desk.

"Yes, we are four this evening," replied Rick.

"Right this way, Mr. Benal. If you will please follow me."

The gentleman led the way into a huge ballroom, where there must have been a hundred tables of ladies and gentlemen all decked out in black tie. Each table appeared to have eight guests. We were led to a table near the front of the room, close to a massive dance floor. There wasn't anyone else at our table yet, even though it appeared to have been set for eight.

"Okay, Rick, this is exciting!" I said, as we were seated.

"It's a small award, but it's our first. So for a new restaurant, it translates into real prestige. These honors are awarded by our peers and the critics who monitor our businesses. Justin should be here too, as we're up for an award tonight."

"Really?" asked Lora. "Oh this is exciting! Have you won?"

"I don't know. No one knows the results until they are announced. Our restaurant has been nominated for three awards: New Restaurant of the Year, Award of Excellence for Menu, Distinguished Restaurant of the Year."

"Wow! That is great, Rick. I'm honored you asked us to accompany you," I said.

"This is very impressive, Rick. It makes me feel very good about my investment!" said Mark.

"Well, we haven't won yet, but keep your fingers crossed. In the meantime, this is a party. The food is free, and there is supposed to be dancing and entertainment. So enjoy it!"

Dinner proved to be a very elegant affair of seven courses, not including dessert. The dress I was wearing didn't have a lot of room for a big meal without a big bulge! Lora had the same problem, but it was fun sampling everything. I noticed that Mark was eating heartily; he didn't have to watch his weight. He took charge of ordering wine and drinks for the table. The bottle he ordered must have been a few hundred dollars, because the wait staff fell over their feet to serve us after that.

The main course was steak, which Lora and I asked for blue. Rick looked at us both and smiled. He knew what that was, and was curious to see if the chef would be able to do that here in Miami. It was common in French culture to have your beef blue, or "bleu" as we said in Montreal. Mark decided to order his the same way, and Rick decided to go along with the table.

Justin still had not shown up, and Rick began to be concerned that he wouldn't get there to accept the award if they won.

"Don't worry, Rick. He'll be here," Lora reassured him.

Sure enough, Justin arrived just then with a winsome blonde with long legs. Lora and I giggled quietly, while Mark and Rick smiled at our private joke.

"Uh Justin, aren't you gay? Who's your date?" Lora asked.

"Hun, she is the eye candy that will chase away the proposals I get from guys I'm not interested in!"

"He's forever fencing off fanboys at culinary events," explained Rick. "It's one of the reasons we usually go as a couple. They leave us alone then."

"But with Rick entertaining a woman, I couldn't be left out, I wanted my own arm candy," said Justin.

The food arrived and was done extremely well. By the time all of our dishes were cleared away, the table swept of crumbs and the wine glasses emptied and cleared, it was close to 10:30. Someone went up to the head table to announce the beginning of the awards. They were apparently giving out roughly twenty different awards here tonight, all for the hospitality industry. That explained the large number of people here.

Most of the awards had nothing to do with Rick, so we chatted quietly at our table and applauded when it was appropriate. They were down to the last five awards, three of which Rick and Justin's restaurant were nominated.

"And the winner for the Award of Excellence for Menu goes to Escalata Steak and Seafood of Atlanta!" announced the emcee.

"Oh my God!" cried Justin as he and Rick jumped up and hugged each other. Rick appeared to be speechless. Justin was pulling him toward the front when he stopped, walked back to the table, and pulled Lora to her feet. He planted a big kiss on her lips before he continued to the podium. Lora was beaming.

Justin was already at the podium, and when Rick arrived they both grasped the award and raised it in the air. The crowd cheered—our table especially. After they said their thank-yous, they returned to the table and sat down. Rick put the award in the center of the table and we were all admiring it.

"Well done, guys," said Mark. "Congratulations!"

"And the winner for the Distinguished Restaurant of the Year goes to Griff's Fine Dining of Tampa Bay!" announced the emcee.

"Oh well, next year, Rick," consoled Lora.

"Folks, the highest honor tonight is our last award. This restaurant started up just a year ago and has set an extremely high standard on service, decor, cuisine, and presentation. They have won acclaim from magazines such as *Santé* in Canada, and the *Michelin Guide*. Miranda Cook is quoted as saying

'They have everything just right; the right blend of color, atmosphere, and great food.' Ladies and gentlemen, the winner of the James Beard Award for Best New Restaurant of the Year goes to … Escalata Steak and Seafood of Atlanta!"

Lora and I screamed a little and the house was on their feet in an ovation to Rick and Justin. They kind of sat stunned for a second. Lora reached over and pulled Rick to his feet, hugging him. He was speechless! He looked at his partner and Justin was the same way. Slowly, it dawned on them they were to go to the podium again. This time on the way there, Rick grabbed Lora's hand and dragged her along with him. She stood there beside him arm in arm with him as he accepted the award. That was way cool!

I glanced over at Mark. He was nodding and smiling, and suitably impressed.

"Hey, I guess I backed the right horse!" he cheered.

"Yeah, no kidding!" I responded.

When the two chefs returned to the table with Lora, Rick swung her around and they did a little dance as everyone was giving them an ovation. When Rick sat down, he pulled Lora onto his lap and held on to her tightly.

"Thank you very much for sharing this with me, darling," he said fervently. "It just wouldn't have been the same without you."

"Well, thanks for agreeing to be my date for the weekend," said Lora.

"Hey, guys, that goes for you too. I'm awfully glad you're here. Let's party, shall we?"

"I think a bottle of champagne is in order!" cried Mark. He motioned over to a waiter and ordered the best bottle the hotel had.

The rest of the night we danced—almost until dawn—and then drove back to the hotel. We were exhausted, but completely pumped because of the high energy night. I suggested a sunrise walk on the beach, and Mark agreed, but Lora and Rick went to bed.

"Falon, did I tell you how stunning you look tonight?" whispered Mark in my ear when the two of them had left.

"You did, thank you. You are pretty handsome yourself. I didn't relish the idea of fighting off the women who were eyeing you all night," I teased him.

"Ah, there were far more men watching you, I believe. You and Lora make quite the pair, don't you? How come she is still single?"

"Well, that's a long story. She's had a rough life. The last husband gave her a son, who is now eight years old. Unfortunately, the ex is a brute. When he started coming home drunk, hitting her middle son, and leering at her eldest daughter, we had to rescue them from the husband until the police arrested him."

"Ouch, that's not fair. She is such a warm, loving person," he said.

"I know. I love her to death. I'm not close to many women. I usually can't stand their petty manipulations and emotional bullshit. Lora isn't like that at all. She's straightforward and honest about her motives. The strength in her is astounding, and her commitment to her kids is amazing, in spite of all the partying. She's a very good mom."

"You asked me a while ago if I had ever thought about having kids," he started. "My answer to you was that I thought about it every time I was with you."

"I remember," I said.

"I am, Falon. I think about having children with you all the time. I think about creating children with you, and how much I want to. You will make an amazing mom too," he said quietly.

We stood there on the beach watching the sun come up. When the first rays of dawn touched the sand, the light fell on our faces.

I was silent after his speech. I still hadn't told him I'd forgiven him. I couldn't quite give voice to that yet. His speech made me feel a little uncomfortable with that knowledge.

As we stood there watching the sun made its debut for the day, we stood arm in arm. Once it had cleared the horizon and shone bright yellow, I turned away from the light and pulled Mark along behind me toward the hotel room and sleep.

Lying in bed, my mind raced. I kept my eyes closed because I had a lot to think about. Mark was breathing gently behind me, but I wasn't convinced he was asleep either as we lay together that morning.

19—Party Time!

I don't like surprises.

I especially don't like surprise birthday parties.

But the following weekend, that is exactly what Lora did. She must have been planning this since she came down, a surprise birthday party for me at the hotel, and she invited everyone!

"How did she manage this?" one might ask. "I don't know!" would be my answer.

The biggest surprise happened when I opened my hotel room door on Saturday morning and she was outside.

"Where did you come from?" I asked.

"Surprise!" she screamed. "I came down for your birthday."

"I didn't think you could afford to come two weekends in a row."

"Mark paid for my flights last weekend, and he did this weekend too. So I could be here."

"Wow!" I said. "Well, come on in—or do you want your room again?"

"I'll leave my bags in the second room, you know in case I can see Rick again."

"It's turning into something, isn't it?" I asked.

"It is turning into something. What I don't know, but it's something," she agreed. "I've planned a birthday party for you."

"You what?"

"You know a birthday party—turning thirty is big."

"How did you do that?"

"I had some key phone numbers, and the rest, as they say, is history," she said glibly.

She was a good friend. Really, she was. I would have loved her for it if I were the kind of person who didn't mind being put on the spot. If I were the kind of person who loved the spotlight, then it would have been wonderful.

"So since you know about it now, you'll have to act surprised so everyone gets to surprise you," said Lora.

"I have to act surprised. Well I can do that."

"Good. I'll get all the preparations done. When you return to the hotel on Friday after work, just pretend it's a normal day, okay?"

"Okay." So when I went back to my hotel room on the date in question, I pretended that it was just another day. Franco spotted me when I walked through the revolving doors of the hotel. He waved me over to the front desk.

"Franco, I am tired and I just want some room service and to go to bed."

"Ms Robertson, there's a phone call waiting for you on the courtesy line in alcove 6," said Franco.

"Thanks, Franco," I said, "Where is alcove six?"

"It's in the bar actually, in the back corner by the bar," he answered.

I walked into the bar; all the lights were off. Everyone was probably hiding. I looked at my watch and it said 7:30 p.m. I pretended to stumble on a chair in the dark as I walked further into the bar.

I made a beeline for the exit sign over the door in the back because it was the only thing I could see. When I got to the back I pushed the handle to open it.

The lights all came on and there was a great cheer in the bar as seventy-five people screamed happy birthday!

I stood there and fashioned the best 'surprised' look on my face I could do. I smiled and said, "Oh you shouldn't have." *Really, you shouldn't have.* Lora was the first to walk forward and hug me. I squinted at her. She knew I hated surprises.

"You did that very well," she whispered.

"You!" I said. "You're responsible, aren't you!" I challenged her to make a fuss.

"Of course," said Lora smugly. "We couldn't let your twenty-ninth birthday go past without a celebration, could we?" She turned to everyone and they all agreed with her.

"You've told them I'm twenty-nine?" I asked her.

"No, but it's on the cake," she answered.

"Great! Now I'm an old Canadian!" I whined.

"You're not old!" she said. "I'm a year older than you and look how fabulous I am!"

She was right. She didn't look her age at all. Neither did I really. It must be the Irish in us. Most people thought I was still in my early twenties. In fact it was the reason I was not taken too seriously sometimes, like that jerk Warren at the restaurant.

After we chatted for a few seconds, I felt better.

"Okay, now I need a drink!" I said.

"Barkeep, pour this woman a drink please!" yelled Lora.

"Coming right up," called Charity. She brought over a pretty cocktail with an umbrella.

"What's this?" I asked. I smelled tequila.

"Oh, it's a special drink just for you," she said. "It's called a Paloma."

Everyone came to congratulate me and hug me. I couldn't believe how many people Lora had roped into this one. Ray came up and apologized for the work this afternoon, but it was the only thing he could think of to keep me at the office while this was being planned.

"You mean that work was a make-work project? I didn't have to do it?" I asked him, but I already knew that.

"Yeah, it's really of no use immediately to *this* project. However, it may be in the future. You came up with some novel ideas that I may take a look at tomorrow."

I playfully punched his shoulder then and he hugged me.

"Good work, Falon. I'm really glad you're part of our team." Ray kissed me, not too boss-like, and disappeared into the pack of guests.

Next to step forward were the Polecats. First Chris, then the other two, and lastly Brandon. Brandon's greeting was suitably passionate while he held me close to him and he kissed me not so chastely.

"Hey, get a room!" someone said from the crowd.

Brandon stuck by a bit while others came up and told me happy birthday. Eventually, everyone was sitting and dinner was being served. Apparently, Lora had arranged for dinner, and the Polecats to play tonight. Lora, Brandon, and I sat together for dinner. But as soon as dessert was over, he disappeared.

It was about five minutes after Brandon disappeared behind the stage that Gwen and Mark arrived. They walked into the bar and straight over to me.

"Falon," Gwen greeted me, "so nice to see you again, and on an occasion of festivities too."

"Is she always this formal?" Lora asked.

"Ah, Lora," said Gwen. "I have heard lots about you. Mark has told me many times about the three of you going out together in Montreal. It's one of his fondest memories."

"Yes, she is. Decorum is very important to her," answered Mark. "Since we're in mixed company," he whispered into my ear, "I shall behave myself only until I can get you alone again."

I couldn't help myself, shivers started going up and down my spine. I directed Gwen and Mark to sit with us, and Mark pulled out the chair closest to me.

"So why are you late?" asked Lora.

"Our flight was late landing here. We were flying in from New Orleans," said Gwen.

"Oh, business or pleasure?"

"Business, we were looking at another property. I'm not sure of that one though," said Mark.

As we were chatting, we didn't notice the band had arrived on stage.

"Ladies and gentlemen," announced Brandon, "welcome to Falon's birthday party! My name is Brandon, and these gentlemen behind me are the Polecats. Tonight, we have been asked to do a special show. We even have a special guest with us." Brandon paused. "But let's get dancing!"

With that, they revved up the night with a series of songs starting with *The Land of 1,000 Dances* by Wilson Pickett, then continued with the Beach Boys and more.

The three of us girls got up dancing our heads off while Mark sat at the table watching. When the tempo changed, Mark cut in on me and we danced. Both Lora and Gwen soon found themselves with partners too. Over Mark's shoulder, I could see Brandon watching us. I could swear he was smoldering. This might be a tricky night to say the least?

The tempo changed again, and this time it was honky-tonk and Southern jazz. Some of it wasn't too danceable, but it was fun to listen to. When the tempo changed again, they soared into a disco revival that had us all laughing while we were doing line dances. Mark was really good at those.

The first set ended and the band came back to our table. We were all crammed into the corner together. The band remembered Lora, of course, but we made introductions for Gwen and Mark.

It got a bit tense for me too. For a few minutes Mark and Brandon silently competed for the chair next to me. Mark changed seats and brought another to my other side. Lora was beside herself trying to not laugh. She did this on purpose because she'd known what would happen!

At one point, when the guys had left the table, I turned to Lora.

"So what am I supposed to do with this competition?"

"Hun, you have to pick one."

"I think I have."

"Did you tell him?"

"No. Not yet. I was waiting for the right moment."

After a while, I saw Lora nudge Rick in the ribs and say, "It's time." He got up and left the bar.

Things settled down a bit as we were all getting into the conversations, but the competition between Mark and Brandon heated up when both of them tried to put their arm across the back of my chair. Brandon backed off that time. I could barely focus on the party. I decided to get up and go for some air. As I was walking out of the bar, Rick saw me and gave me a big hug.

"You can't leave!" he said, "March yourself back in there!" he grinned.

I turned around and went back to the table where Lora was sitting.

I turned around to watch Rick walk into the bar to supervise the cake delivery. Brandon and Mark were standing by the door watching.

Wow, have my chickens come home to roost!

I had to face this competition that I had created. *I have to grow a pair of.... ovaries ... and face the music.*

The cake rolled in and everyone started singing "happy birthday" to me. I was surrounded by Lora, Rick, Mark, Brandon, and Gwen.

"Come on, blow out the candles!"

I huffed and puffed and blew them all out. It was a lot! A big cheer went up and the band got back up on stage.

"I have to leave for a few minutes," said Mark, leaning down to me.

"Why?"

"I cannot tell you." he grinned.

Mark and Gwen left. Everyone else was having a massively good time. The band was really cooking tonight. When I got back to the table after dancing, Lora came over and told me that Mark had left me a message. She winked at me.

"Okay, what's the message, Lora?" I asked.

"He'll see you later upstairs was all he said," she replied, and her face was split with a huge grin. "So are we gonna have another wonderful foursome?" she asked.

"Are you bringing Rick?" I asked.

"Hmmm, Rick. I think I could fall for him, Falon," Lora replied as she danced her way to the dance floor.

The music stopped and Brandon stepped up to the mic.

"Ladies and gentlemen, it's time to bring out our special guest tonight. Please give a huge round of applause for the Tom Cats!" cried Brandon.

"You're kidding!" I screamed.

Bobby and the Tom Cats strutted out on stage right then and spun the crowd into a frenzy with my two favorite songs. Brandon came and danced with me on the first, and Rick cut in on the second. The whole band, Lora, and a bunch of others, including Ray, were up on the dance floor having a blast. The Tom Cats paused for a minute after these songs and Bobby came to the mic:

"Falon, are you out there?" he asked the audience.

"Yeah, she's over here!" called Charity.

"Falon, since you're such a big fan, how would you like to be the first to hear a new song I'm playing with? It's called *Jump, Jive, An' Wail* by Louis Prima.

The crowd cheered their answer, so Bobby turned to his band and said, "Hit it!" Soon they were cooking on the new piece of music and everyone was jiving along with them.

"What an amazing gift! Okay, that was pretty cool. Thanks, Lora!"

"Hun, I had help, but I knew this would be the icing on the cake."

The Tom Cats could only stay for a few songs, but before they left Bobby came and thanked us for the invitation to the birthday party. Lora grinned seductively and Bobby winked.

When the second set finished, the boys were back at the table, and a round of shooters appeared again. Brandon decided that he would make his move.

"Falon, how about a little birthday love later?" he asked

"Mmmm, Brandon, I don't think so," I said.

"Why?"

"Because I have to grow up and stop playing around. I want a family and I have to settle down to do that."

Brandon got quiet then. He turned my chair around so that it faced him directly. There was no seduction, no lewdness, no pressure. He just kissed me gently.

Then he got down on one knee. The rest of the band stopped what they were doing and gathered around our table. Brandon reached behind him and pulled out a small box. I felt myself gulp and swallow. *Oh no.*

"Falon, I would love to have a family with you. Ever since we talked about it, I can't stop thinking about it. I can't stop thinking about us and how well we fit together. I've fallen madly in love with you and want to share my world with you forever. Would you consider having me as a husband?"

I was stunned. "Brandon, did you just ask me to marry you?"

"Yes, I did."

Oh my! I wasn't thinking this way with him. He was fun, sexy, nice to have around, and I had some feelings for him, but my feelings for Mark completely eclipsed that.

"Are you sure?" I asked.

"As sure as I am of anything," said Brandon.

A few moments passed …. the room fell absolutely silent. Not good.

"I'm sorry, Brandon. I was giving your proposal serious thought. But much as I really like you, I don't believe we could make it work. My life isn't here in Georgia. I won't be staying very long, and I just don't see myself being a band girl."

As I spoke, the resolve in me strengthened and a calm came over me again. This was my choice and it was clear.

Brandon's face fell in disappointment, but he didn't argue or beg—for which I was grateful. It would have been a terrible scene if it had devolved into that. Instead, the guys clapped me on the back and hugged me so long. It was understood I wasn't going to be part of the band. Brandon gently kissed me goodnight.

"Brandon, save that wonderful heart of yours for a Southern girl who will be everything to you and to who you're everything," I whispered into his ear.

"Falon, I will, but she had better be very like you, because you are my everything," he replied sadly.

"No, I'm not, Brandon. I was a diversion and some well-spent time. It was never meant to be, because I was never going to be staying."

The band resumed their music and performed another set. Around 2:00 a.m. the party was shut down by the hotel staff and everyone went home, except for Rick. Rick came over to sit with Lora, and they were cooing at each other. When the three of us got up to leave, everything was quiet. In the elevator, Lora and Rick were so into each other they didn't even notice me.

When we got to our floor, we said goodnight to each other and I went into my bedroom, leaving the second room for Lora and Rick again. I shut the door behind me and walked over to the bed.

"Well, this isn't a fun finish to my party," I grumbled.

"What's wrong with the ending?" came a voice out of the dark.

"Mark, you're here!"

"I said I would see you upstairs," he answered. He walked over to me and wrapped his arms around me. "I'm here to give you my birthday present," he murmured into my hair.

He took me by the hand and led me to the bed and slowly undressed me, dropping each item on the floor as he went. When I was standing there before him in my birthday suit, he smiled in the moonlight. He then took my head between his fingers and kissed me lightly at first, then deeply.

He efficiently stripped and stepped back to embrace me in seconds. Our skin touched the whole length of our bodies, and the fire we felt sizzled. He touched me everywhere with his hands, bringing tingles and shivers to my skin. Picking me up in his arms, he walked over to the bed.

There were no gymnastics this time, no exciting new poses, or new sensations. But there was a deep connection. We made sweet love, slowly, passionately, deeply.

He held me at the brink and then gently let my climax wash me as we came together as one. It was beautiful. We didn't even speak. Communicating with movement and touch, we "talked." I took up one of his hands and tried to do what Mark had done to me—the hand dance. Mark exhaled lightly as the sensations took him.

I snuggled into his shoulder as he held me there. I was listening to the steady rhythm of his heart. I was at peace.

I soon fell asleep cocooned in his arms.

When I woke the next morning, Mark was gone. I thought that was a bit odd, he'd never done that before. When I got up and went out to the living room, there was a note on the table: Mark had to run an errand and would be back.

I got dressed and knocked on Lora and Rick's door. They might have been asleep still; no one answered. I thought they made a nice-looking couple, but I didn't know if there was anything permanent about it. Lora's kids were the center of her life. She'd told me that when the youngest was grown perhaps she would consider taking another husband again. But not until then. She wouldn't ever risk her kids again with a bad relationship.

I went back to my room and made some horrible coffee as I waited for Mark to return. Lora joined me for coffee not long afterwards.

"Did you have a good night with Rick?" I asked her. "And where is he?"

"Oh, he's still asleep. Yes, it was wonderful. We fit together very well. He's adventurous, fun, and serious too," said Lora. "Oh, Falon, I want to keep him."

"How would you do that?"

"I don't know," she said. "Perhaps I can move here with the kids."

"You'll figure it out if it's important enough. You always do."

A couple of hours later my phone rang. When I answered it, Mark's voice was on the other end.

"Good morning, love," said Mark. "Did you sleep well?"

"Good morning, Mark," I answered. Lora's face showed an "oh!" expression when she heard Mark's name. "I slept like a baby being cradled."

"Now that I've heard your voice, my day is perfect."

"Are you coming back soon?" I said.

"I had hoped to, but I've gotten caught in something else. I'll be there in a little while though. Can I come and find you?"

"Of course!" I said. "Why would you ask?"

"Just wanted to make sure," he said.

"I'll see you when you get here, then. Lora's still here. We're going to hang around the pool today, I think," I said to him. I looked at Lora and she was nodding in agreement.

"I'll come up and see you when I get free, then," he said.

I hung up the phone and looked back at Lora. She was smiling widely. She knew I had strong feelings for Mark.

"So where do we wait on the Texan?" she asked me.

"It appears he'll be here soon and will meet us at the pool."

"Well, let's get going, then!"

Rick was dressed and ready to leave when we went back into the living room. He had to get a change of clothes and run some errands today. Asking when he and Lora could get together again later today, he kissed her goodbye as he walked out the door.

We went down for brunch and then changed for the pool. Grabbing books, towels, cover-ups, and lotion, we made our way up to the pool for an afternoon of relaxation.

It was just after lunch when Mark arrived at the pool. He actually looked tired when he came and sat down on a lounge chair next to us. I was going to order a drink for him, but he said he just wanted to get some sleep.

"Are you alright?" I asked him, concerned a little by this change in his energy level.

"Yeah, I'm fine, just a little jet-lagged because of all the flying this past week. I think I've crossed five time zones twice! What time is it?"

"It's two o'clock actually. Would you like a drink with us?" I asked.

"Maybe, something cool would be nice. I'll find a lounge in the shade here close to you girls and have a nap, if that's okay?"

"That works," I said. I ordered some drinks for all of us.

When the drinks arrived, Mark was asleep in the shade beside me. We let him sleep until dinner. Lora and I kept reading and chatting for the rest of that afternoon, relaxing in the sunshine. Around dinner time, I nudged Mark awake.

"Hey sleepyhead, wake up!" I called softly.

"Mmmm, Falon, is that you?" he asked groggily.

I got up, went over to his chair and kissed him gently. His arms wrapped themselves around me even with his eyes closed. A smile appeared on his lips. It was a tasty-looking smile, so I had to kiss it again. This time his eyes opened and he gazed at me. They were warm brown today.

"Hey, it's dinnertime. Would you like to join us?" I asked.

"I'll accompany you for sure."

We gathered up our things and went back down to the dining room for dinner. We ordered steaks, baked potatoes, and veg for all three of us. As in Miami, when Lora asked for hers blue, the server was a little puzzled. She had to explain that she wanted it almost raw—just lightly seared on the outside and bloody on the inside. I think I saw the server shudder at that description. When I ordered my steak the same way, Mark smiled.

When the steaks arrived, we all dug in with gusto.

"That's very good," he said. "I've never seen anyone else eat a steak like this, except you two."

"It's fairly common in Montreal," Lora explained.

"Figures!" said Mark.

"Lora, what time is your flight back?" I asked her.

"You're leaving tonight?" Mark asked.

"Yes, I have to go home to my babies. I can't stay down here and play forever. It's 11:45 p.m.," she answered.

"Okay, I'll drive you to the airport at 9:30, then," I offered.

"No, Falon. Rick is picking me up and taking me," said Lora.

"When will he be here?" Mark asked.

"It should be soon."

Sure enough, Rick came walking through the door of the dining room and made a beeline for our table. Mark and Rick greeted each other, but it was the greeting between Rick and Lora that was interesting. They stared at each other for quite a while before he took both her hands and pulled her into his arms. Their kiss was hot enough that there was steam coming off them!

After dinner, Rick accompanied Lora upstairs to help her pack her bags. Mark and I didn't expect them down very soon, so we stayed at the table and had another drink.

A little while later, Rick and Lora were back downstairs again with her bags. The four of us walked her to the front door and said goodbye, as Rick called for his car from the valet parking. While the porter was putting her bags in the car, I leaned in the passenger side window and hugged her.

"Thanks so much for my party, and for being here," I said with a catch in my throat.

"I know you hate surprises!" said Lora, "So I couldn't resist!"

"Bitch!" I said as I hugged her.

"Of course! But you wouldn't expect otherwise, now would you?"

"No, and I would have been terribly disappointed if someone hadn't done something I guess," I admitted.

"Bye, love, take care. We'll see you in Montreal in a few weeks again, no?" Lora prompted.

"Yes, I should be back in the middle of September. Until then, keep a close eye on Armand. I don't want him going through my drawers!"

Lora scrunched up her nose. "Ewww! Has he?"

"I've found some things out of place, but I can't say for sure. You know, perhaps we should stop using him so much," I suggested.

"Nah, he'd never be happy then. He likes being used. He thinks he'll score as a payment. 'Sides, he's always waiting for the opportunity to get us just drunk enough that we won't notice him trying to fuck us!" Lora screamed.

Lora got into the car as the two of us laughed at the honesty of that statement, and Rick pulled away from the door. Lora was hanging out the window waving crazily while I was waving from the sidewalk.

Mark and I walked back to my room.

20—A Life Decision Made

"Falon," a voice whispered in my mind.

I was dreaming, an erotic sensual dream. Mark was in it. He was all over me, his hands caressing every inch of my body sending shivers through my limbs. He was inside me, around me, through me. I could feel an electrical current traveling from his fingers through my skin. He was arousing me so much without doing very much. I wanted to stay here forever. I strained to stay asleep, because I didn't want the dream to end, and I knew I was waking up.

"Falon," said the voice again.

This time it seemed distant and whispered. I sensed longing in it and sorrow. I was floating around the hotel room looking for the voice. I looked in the living room, but all I saw was a shadowy figure that didn't seem to coalesce into anything.

"Falon, come back to me," it said again.

Then I looked in the bathroom and still no one was around, so I floated into the bedroom. I saw myself lying on the bed asleep. That shadowy figure was behind me. I knew I needed to wake up from this dream.

I opened my eyes and Mark was there lying behind me. I must have fallen asleep on him last night. I didn't remember him coming to bed. But that dream … my body still ached with him; I could feel him inside me still; another sense of déjà vu.

"Hi," he said quietly.

At that moment, I suddenly noticed his scent. I rolled over to face him. I was sniffing the air like a dog trying to catch something I thought was there. When I reached him, his hand took mine and he pulled me to him.

"What is that scent? I asked him, "It's you but different."

I turned around and he was right there. I looked at his eyes; they had those gold circles swirling around his irises. When his touch brought me back to reality, I knew I had become lost in those eyes. His hand was touching the side of my face and he was stroking my cheek.

"Sorry for startling you." His voice was rough with desire. I rolled into his embrace and leaned against his body. There I was again, feeling like I was home. That sense of fitting and belonging was so strong that I sighed and relaxed against him. We stayed there for a few minutes, me leaning against him, his arms around me, and his cheek resting on the top of my head.

Finally he pulled himself away. "Falon, we need to finish that conversation," he said.

"Haven't you told me everything?" I asked. "You've told me a lot. What else is there? I know you said that the bite wasn't a death blow though. That I had to consent. Consent to what?"

"If you love me as I love you, you can consent to a ritual that will turn you into one of us. The ritual requires sex. I take a drug which chemically alters my venom. Then my venom transfers some of my immortality to you through my bite. That leaves me vulnerable until the conclusion of the ritual. The venom actually kills you and then brings you back. Through orgasm, both venom and seed are put in your body. Your arousal makes your body respond to the venom to produce the correct enzymes to break down the toxic elements of the venom."

"How do we know if it works?" I asked.

"Seventy-two hours after orgasm, you get bitten. If the wound heals quickly, you're becoming immortal."

"And if not?"

"If not, then we have to administer a counteragent drug to prevent you from dying."

"Oh."

Now my curiosity was getting the better part of me. I might as well ask my questions since he was in lecture mode.

"How old are you?" I asked.

"Seven hundred and fifty years old. I'm basically the same age as you relative to my elders."

"Do you change into other things or just change your appearance?" I asked.

"I cannot change into anything else. But there are others who have the ability to shapeshift into other animals."

"You're much stronger than I am," I said.

"Yes, I have the strength of about three human males."

"Why me? I mean, if we're off limits to you, why did you even start something with me all those years ago?" I asked.

"That's an excellent question. That's a bit of a story," he answered.

"I'm listening, and we have all night…"

"Ah, a weakness of mine. I like people. I like being around people. Some of them are very cool. If I pretend to be just like them, I can go undetected for years. In Montreal, I found a culture that allowed me to be with people in a way I hadn't in years. They were alive, vivacious, fun-loving, and life-affirming. I was drawn to the small communities of alter-egos on the bulletin boards because I could be who I was without detection. I could be a vampire and everyone would only think it was a fictional persona. I could be the Grand Master because that was an alter-ego people would accept.

"After communicating for some months, I wanted to see who these people were. So that is why I was at that bar that night. It was the first time in a long time I was among people, the first time I dared to go out into the social life in person. It was exciting to sit there, in the corner, without anyone really noticing me—until you walked through the door. You noticed me. You saw me. You weren't supposed to be able to, but you did."

He stopped then at this point and fell silent. I somehow knew to stay quiet, wait, and I would get the rest of the story.

"I had been sitting there, using our skills of shadow to keep myself from being noticeable," he continued after a minute. "It works on most people, probably ninety-nine percent of the population. But on you … it didn't. You were looking directly at me, seeing me, seeing through me to my soul. That was one of my clues. At the same time, there was an unmistakable attraction, like you were pulling a rope tied to my heart. It freaked me out. I thought I had been discovered. That you had seen the effect, but still saw me too. I didn't know what to do. Discovery means trouble, usually."

"Clue to what?" I asked.

"When you followed your husband to the other side, I relaxed a little. Maybe it was a fluke. I followed you and sat in another corner watching you. I couldn't help myself, I was fascinated by you, like a moth to a flame. I was using shadow skill in that room, and whether or not it showed I do not know, but you didn't see me again.

"Then you left with a guy to dance in the other room. I followed you again and watched the two of you dancing. I felt all my aggressiveness coming out, my fangs distended, and the only thought through my head was 'She's mine, get your hands off her!' I interrupted and asked you to have a drink with me. As I got close to you, your scent practically intoxicated me. Your scent was stimulating me more than had ever happened before. When I was close to you, I let my shadow skills drop slowly so that the people around me didn't get startled. I tapped you on your shoulder and you turned to face me.

"I felt the floor drop from under my feet at that moment. It took everything I had to keep myself under control. I wanted you. My body ached for you. These were feelings I didn't understand because they had never happened before. That was another clue."

"To what?" I asked.

"To the possibility that you were one of us, unturned," he answered. I stared at him in shock.

"Then you came back fifteen minutes later. You appeared to be looking for someone, and I hoped it was me. I was wrapped in shadow again, you should not have been able to see me. So when you went to the bar, I understood the initial moment we saw each other was special somehow. I walked up behind you, dissipating the shadow as I went. By the time I was at the bar, I was solid and you would see me fully. I didn't want to frighten you, so I spoke quietly."

"And you introduced yourself," I said. "Your voice was like smooth butter, and sensual beyond anything. I felt shivers when you spoke. I remember turning toward you and seeing your eyes for the first time. I felt like they were pools and I wanted to fall into them."

"You fascinated me more than anyone—my kind or human," he continued. "I was drawn even more to you, and was emotionally tied to you before the end of that conversation. I didn't want you to return to your friends, I wanted you to leave with me right there and then. But I couldn't do that. It was forbidden.

"So I made a point of contacting you on the boards. We started a relationship there that couldn't happen in real life. I could have you there, in that world of make-believe. Grand Master could fall in love with Leopard Lady. They could make passionate love, and flirt in public. Our affair gave me a reason to stay online, because I waited for you to be there.

"The day you invited me to your house and outlined what you had planned, I knew it would be difficult to keep my distance. Being impartial around you was very hard, but to know what your goal was, it made my heart soar. I knew I had to try.

"When I arrived and you were so business-like, I thought I might make it. However, when we sat on the sofa together and our hands touched, I couldn't help my energy from reaching out to you, could not prevent myself from claiming you. Kissing you that first time was the most exquisite moment. I was completely intoxicated by your scent, your skin, your softness. I wanted to touch every part of you, wanted to own you completely. I wanted to rip your clothes off and plunge myself so deep within you and make you mine."

I could see the strong emotions battling on his face, could sense the memories moving inside him, as they moved inside me. As he was recounting these memories, I was living them again too. I was feeling that flare of passion again. I remembered it very well. I waited again for fear he might stop. After swallowing, he continued.

"When your reaction to me was easily as strong, it inflamed me. I had to touch you. I had to have you. When you kept playing with fire, I couldn't stop. I was surprised that my touch brought you to orgasm, and honored that I was the one to give you that. I had to follow you upstairs because I was like a caveman going to claim his woman. I'm not sure you could have stopped me. It's a good thing you wanted me as much as I wanted you.

"When your ex walked in the door at the moment he did, he witnessed me claiming my lifemate. I wasn't finished by any means."

"Hmmm, I remember your eyes having gold rings swirling in them," I said with a smile.

"I could see his rage, and that sobered me up quickly, because he was a real threat to you physically. He wouldn't be able to hurt me, but you couldn't know that just yet. When he lunged for you, I was up and had him by the throat and was pushing him up against the wall before he knew what had happened. For a second there, he had fear in his eyes. Then it was covered with self-righteous indignation. I let him go and he tried to push me. I easily stopped him and quietly spoke so that you wouldn't hear me. I intended on killing him if he so much as touched a hair on your head again. I only relaxed when he left that night."

"Wow, I hadn't known that was why he went downstairs. I just thought it was because he was disgusted," I said.

"No, I told him, compelled him to go down with the warning that if he came back up I would break him in two," said Mark. "He had no trouble believing me."

"Mark," I hesitated, "…where does this leave us? If you're forbidden to be with humans, then what does that mean for our relationship?"

"That's the point, Falon," he answered me. "I don't believe you're only human. I think you're one of us, unturned. We all have to turn. The strength of our bond, the fact you could see through my shadow, these are indicators you are supposed to be one of us."

"Oh wow," I said. "I agree, my attraction to you was instant, and all-consuming. I've never had that before or since. When I met you, I couldn't keep my hands off you when you asked to kiss me."

"I want to turn you so that we can be together."

"You mean we could have a life together? We could get married, love, live together, have children?" I asked him. "I thought you told me you wanted to have children with me"

"Yes, all that."

"One problem," I said. "I had my tubes tied a few years ago."

"When you get remade, your whole body will be restored, including your reproductive system."

"How do you get into my rooms without keys? And how do you know when I need you?" I asked.

"The first is easy, I have a key. I just go up the stairs much faster than the elevator can travel. The second is directly related to how closely we are connected. I can sense when you're in danger, because I can hear you even at great distances. When I'm close to you, I can hear your thoughts."

"Hear me? Do you mean my speaking voice?" I asked.

"No, I hear your thoughts—and your emotions. If you're scared, I feel your fear and can find you. If you're angry, I feel it and can find you. Your emotions are like a homing beacon to me."

"Did you sense my fear when I was out for dinner with that cretin?" I asked him.

"Yes. Your fear has a very salty taste, and it's tinged with an acrid smell," he explained. "But more importantly, your aura changes, acting like a searchlight for me."

"Salty? I guess that makes sense. But doesn't everyone have emotions? How can you hear mine?" I asked.

"Because I love you," he said simply.

"I love you too. I guess I never stopped loving you. So where do we go now?" I asked.

"That's up to you," he said honestly. "I've defied my elders again. Our code is strong, and the consequences are severe for breaking the code. They have the right to kill me if they believe I have put our community at risk of detection."

"How would they kill you?"

"Chop off my head," he answered.

"Grisly!" I said. "But surely there is such a thing as an exception? I mean, how have you escaped their notice now? What about Gwen?"

"Gwen believes that you deserve to know the whole truth. She also believes that our love is true and eternal. She has put her own life on the line to help us, to help me find you. She too would be killed for breaking the rules. She really is a good sister."

"Do you have other siblings?" I asked.

"Yes, our kind breeds. However, it happens rarely now. The movie vampire simply bites someone to create a new one. We do it the old-fashioned way. But our bodies don't remain fertile for the length of time we live. Our females don't have many children."

"All those years ago, you said you had asked to have me join your family. What did that mean?" I asked.

"Simply a type of marriage. You would become my wife, take a vow of secrecy to protect our clan, our kind, and consent to be turned."

"Here's a practical question: you live in Houston, I live in Montreal. Would you move back to Montreal?" I asked.

"I would go wherever you are. I do not intend on hiding anymore. I don't believe you will risk me or my kind. I trust you implicitly and they will too. Would you take the vow of secrecy willingly?"

"I will do anything you need when we get married," I said.

"It's what I would hope for, yes."

He was right, I did know, I just couldn't see. Now I saw. This was my Zisis, my Mark, the one who had rescued me so long ago. The one I felt at home with, complete with. The one I wanted to spend the rest of my life with. He wanted me too. Was there ever any other answer to that question?

"Yes, I consent and I will marry you," I answered him.

He had been holding his breath—so to speak—for those few seconds. He let it out then, with a huge smile on his face. He was off the bed in an instant, lifting me effortlessly and spinning me around in his arms. I was getting dizzy!

"Stop it! I can't see anymore!" I cried.

He put me down on the bed again, down on one knee in front of me. I could feel the tears welling in my eyes at this moment. He reached into his pocket and pulled out a small brown velvet box. Opening it, he got down on both knees in front of me and held it out to me.

"Falon Robertson, will you be my mate?" he asked me with a thick voice.

"Mark Chisholm, only if you will be mine," I answered.

"Forever and a day," he responded.

"Forever and a day," I responded.

He took the simple band from the box and slipped it around my finger.

"We are now family. For the rest of your days, I will be by your side and I will love you as much in a hundred years as I do right now," he spoke quietly.

"What if I don't live a hundred years?"

"Falon, try not to ruin a perfect moment, okay?"

"Okay."

He took me into his arms then, and we held each other for a long while. When he made love to me that morning, it was with a depth I had not yet felt. He gave me his entire self. He held absolutely nothing back. We were one person. He let me feel through him the transcendent moment he felt. We floated from sheer joy, and were made weightless in a peace I had never felt before. The bite? It hurt, but then like all pain it faded with the euphoria of the drug in his venom. My body responded to him like a violin did to a virtuoso.

When we were satiated, we both fell asleep in each other's arms.

It was some hours later I woke up still nestled into his shoulder with his arm holding me close to his body.

I looked up and watched him sleep. Looking at the clock, I saw we had been asleep for over ten hours. That was unusual for both of us.

"Love…" I gently stroked his cheek and brushed the hair back from his face. "Love," I whispered into his ear.

"Mmmm, I just had the most amazing dream," Mark crooned.

"Yeah?" I asked. "What about?"

"A beautiful woman and the most amazing sex I've ever had," he answered me. Looking into my eyes, he was smiling.

"That wasn't a dream," I answered.

"How's your shoulder?" he asked.

"It's fine," I said. "Should there be a problem?"

"I don't know. But I emptied myself into you. I detected a difference too, once my venom was ejected fully. There was a hollow feeling in my fangs. It was weird. That coupled with a sudden weakness I've never felt before."

"Do you still feel weak?" I asked. "I felt the venom. It stung a bit this time. The euphoria came and took the pain away. But it was different," I agreed.

He took his hand and felt my forehead.

"You're a little warm," he said in response. "Yes, the weakness is still there, so don't ask me to move waterbeds, okay?"

"Is that normal?" I chuckled. "The fever I mean."

"I don't know. I have never done this before. How do you feel? Any different?"

I thought about that. Did I feel different? Maybe. I did feel a little feverish.

"I feel like my body is fighting off something," I answered. "Perhaps it's fighting off the venom."

"We need to wait seventy-two hours. Then we can test it."

We spent the next three days lying around in bed and watching movies. Lying in each other's arms, feeding each other from a room service tray, enjoying each other's company—the luxury of life. When our seventy-two hours were up, he collected me on the bed and took my hand.

"Are you ready?" he asked me earnestly.

"Ready for what?"

"The test. I need to create a small wound," he explained.

"Go ahead, I trust you."

He took my hand and gently bit into the fleshy part. The bite was deep, and blood welled up immediately and dripped down my wrist. Mark reached for some tissue to wipe the blood away. By the time he did I watched the wound close over and disappear as though it had never been.

I gasped.

I experienced a new sensation: I could feel Mark's heart in my chest as if it were my own. I placed my hand on his chest, and sure enough the two heart beats were synchronized.

"Did you know that would happen?" I asked him in wonder.

"No." But he was smiling. "You will start seeing things differently, hearing things differently, and now our lovemaking will be even grander."

"Even better sex? That's not possible," I said, shaking my head.

"Yes, my love, because neither of us has to hold back anymore," he said with meaning in his eyes. "You will have more stamina too."

Whatever else was to come, it could wait. I had him back. He was with me, and I was with him. We could face it together.

Excerpt from Book 3

IMMORTAL PERIL

Chapter 1

Justin wanted to do something special for our restaurant's New Year's Eve celebration. After winning the James Beard award last August, the restaurant had become busier than ever, so we hired a full-time manager to handle the day-to-day operations and increase our chef staff. Justin still set the menus and designed the cuisine, but there were now two executive chefs who did all the work.

I was feeling something was missing for the celebrations, and it was Lora. After that amazing visit in October for the Hallowe'en party, I was missing her terribly. I realized I was rather addicted to her already. Her scent, the feel of her skin, how she loved me … I didn't want to be without her anymore.

Phone calls didn't cut it either. I'd tried to bury myself in the business, which helped a lot. However, when I was alone, it was empty. I missed her smile, her lovely eyes, and especially her wicked sense of humor. I loved the way she flirted with not-so-subtle innuendo and was not afraid to back it up with action.

So many women flirted, suggested, but when it came down to it, they were not prepared to do what they proposed. Lora always followed through, so far at least. She was as adventurous as I was—she hadn't said no to anything yet.

Maybe I should give her a call and see if I could get her down to Atlanta again. I knew she was on a tight budget, and raising three kids was difficult on a single parent's salary. I had no problem paying for her travel; after all, I was comfortably well off. I could always bring them all down and then have Mama Anita babysit them at night when I took Lora out. But maybe she would rather stay with her kids.

I'd offer her either option. It didn't matter to me, as long as I got to see her. Pulling her business card out, I gave her a call.

"Lora O'Reilly speaking, how may I help you today?" came her lovely voice.

"The accent isn't as noticeable today," I replied. "I kind of miss it."

"Rick! Oh, what a pleasure hearing from you!" she exclaimed. "I was just thinking about you and our last phone call."

"That's nice to hear!" I said, as a memory of that call flashed in my mind, bringing back the heat I'd felt during our telephone sex. "I was hoping to convince you to come down again to Atlanta. It has been a while since we saw each other."

"I didn't know we were 'seeing each other,'" Lora said. A little nervous butterfly started flapping in my gut. *Why?* "That's still a little way off for me. It's what, six weeks away?"

"Why don't we start seeing each other?" I countered.

"Rick, I live twelve hundred miles away. How do we see each other?" Lora asked. "I'm not into long distance relationships. They never work out."

"Lora, I'm not going to beat around the bush. I'm a wealthy man," I said. "I want to be with you as often as possible, and I'm willing to pay for your travel expenses or fly to see you. I just can't let you go. You've touched my soul. You've captured my heart. Not to mention the sex with you is, well, I don't want to be with another woman, ever. I want to see where this can go. Where we can go."

"Oh," said Lora.

The line went silent for a minute.

"Lora? Are you still there?"

"Sorry, I was thinking about what you said," she said. "Okay, here's what I think: I want to see where this goes too. I'm just concerned about my kids, and how this is all going to work. I don't want to bring another man into their lives if it's not going somewhere. Does that make sense? And their father is an asshole, so I have to deal with that too."

"Yes, it does. So, can we see if it goes somewhere?" I asked. "I felt so much for you so quickly, I need to know if my mind is leading me on or if it is real."

"Agreed. Let's see if this chemistry between us is really a thing," she suggested.

I let out the breath I didn't know I was holding.

"Okay, Justin and I are having a big party event for New Year's," I said. "Would you like to come down for the New Year's Eve party? You can bring the kids, have a vacation with them here. I can book flights for you. You can come down after work, on Friday night or even Saturday morning once the kids are off school."

"As always, I have to find out what the kids' father is doing. I will get back to you as soon as I can. Okay?"

"Good," I answered. "I look forward to it."

"Bye!"

What's Next?

Book 3 — Immortal Peril

The family is not happy!

- Falon and Mark end up in perilous situations.
- Lora and Rick's friendship develops some steam.
- Lora uses her occult connections to dig into the past.
- And don't forget, Kansas is Tornado country!

About The Author

Linda Ashton Trott

Ms Trott, a native of Montreal, Canada, currently lives in the nation's capital with her husband of twenty-four years, their four cats, and eight Japanese Koi.

When not writing, Ms Trott can be found in their backyard relaxing by the pond or editing her husband's stories.

Ms Trott has always had an interest in all things supernatural, the occult, UFOs, aliens, and the paranormal. It seemed natural to combine one or more of these elements into a unique universe in which to tell interesting stories.

These are not children's stories. "It's funny, I never sat down with the intention of writing Adult books," Linda once said. "But here they are. I wanted to express physical love honestly without cutesy acronyms and vague names."

These stories contain explicit language and hot, steamy sex scenes that will leave you panting.

Books In This Series

The Immortal Stories Series

The Immortals are a race of beings that came to Earth many tens of thousands of years ago. Their stories stretch across time and have become woven into the history of humans. Their society is hidden from humans even though they live among them. Forbidden from developing romantic liaisons with humans, some break the rules and form close bonds and get married. But this always comes with consequences.

1 - Immortal Desire

One immortal and one human.

As Zisis's world collides with Falon's, she is left to cope and deal with the blowback. Their love affair is erotic, passionate, and stirs the soul, but it is ill-fated. This is a story of romance, heartbreak, hardship, and survival. The sex is hot and steamy, the highs euphoric, and the lows devastating.

2 - Immortal Fulfillment

What a twist! What has Mark done?

After a nasty life twist has her rethinking a relationship with her Texan, Falon needs to decide which direction to go. Is she back to square one? Certainly not! Between hurricanes, hot tub invites, and road trips with hot, sexy guys, there is plenty of action and adventure.

3 - Immortal Peril

The Family is NOT happy!

Lora meets Rick, a talented dessert chef in an up-and-coming restaurant in Atlanta, Georgia, while visiting her best friend, Falon, who is on contract work there. Lora and Rick hit it off in ways she can't believe—one hot weekend in Miami and she can't get him out of her mind. So, when invited to Atlanta again, this time by Rick, she doesn't hesitate!

When Mark disappears without a trace, Falon is left to find out what happened.

4 - Immortal Victory

Out of the fire and into the frying pan!

Falon gets out of one problem only to find herself in danger again. An ancient enemy is targeting the immortals and will stop at nothing to eliminate them. Dodging assassins and traps, Falon decides to end homelessness, one person at a time.

Her BFF Lora discovers that true love sex generates magical energy while she looks for her ancestors.

Gwen finds a partner in Andrews.

5 - Immortal Hunt

Having just survived a coordinated attack from an ancient enemy, the immortals rejoice and celebrate their success. Attention turns toward locating their ancestors when a news item catches Lora's attention and gives her a very important clue to finding them. The immortals are off on a great adventure to distant places. Pirates, witches, time travel, spooky castles, and volcanic caves are some of the encounters happening this time. Don't miss out on the adventure!

6 - Immortal Nexus

New is old, and old is new

Surely, saving a coven of witches from a pocket dimension would be a highlight in life. But it's not. The immortals return home to everyday life; family, moving, school, raising teens, and of course, spicy lovemaking.

We meet a new character with a deep past. And when a new couple moves in across the street, Falon notices some familiar characteristics. She makes it her mission to meet the new neighbors.

Family matters are front and center in this story. The close-knit group of immortals is becoming a family, and some stories need sharing like Andrews' tale of being hired by aliens.

Justin and Rick finally open the new restaurant. It was a New Year's Eve celebration with a bang!

7 - Immortal Generation — Coming 2023

Short Stories

First Contact: An Immortal Origin Story

The Immortal's Origin Story started 33,000 years ago, when they arrived on Earth. *First Contact* follows the story of how the immortals meet the first humans and what happens when they interact and live together.

Praise for the Series

What are readers saying about this new series?

"Yet again I've got an ARC for this author and I've got to say that these books just get better and better. I loved this one [Book 6] and it is my favourite so far out of the series. There is now so many new people with there own stories that I don't think it will get boring any time soon. My favourite couple were Falon and Mark but I have quickly fallen in love with Margaret and Abeo and I didn't see the twist and turns right at the end. Brilliant book by a brilliant author."

... Sam ***** Amazon

"Linda Ashton Trott has a real gift for crafting intricate sex scenes that are highly charged and also entirely believable. She really brings you into the bedroom in a joyful way. The will-they-or-won't-they story keeps you wondering, right up to the plot twist at the end, which sets readers up for Book 2."

... Amy **** Amazon

"Ohhhhh! This book was good! Hot hot scenes with enough of a story in between to keep you hooked. We all need to

become Leopard Ladies! Nice quick read. Can't wait to read book 2 of the series!"

... Josée **** Goodreads

"Brilliant book loved the storyline and I couldn't put it down once I started. I loved the characters and got really absorbed in to their lives and feelings.

all I can say is Wow I loved every part of it (#3). I'm really sad that the book ended the way it did as I wanted to carry on reading and finding out what was going to happen. I love this series and all the characters. Hopefully there should be another one."

... Sam ***** Amazon

"Picking up where the first book ended, this installment of the series was the heroine's journey of self-discovery in order to make the right decisions for her, something I really enjoyed!

This book was sexy, fun and the character development was great! Ioved how the heroine slowly took back control of her life and found empowerment in her spontaneity."

...Nikita **** Goodreads

"wow! amazing, fast paced and enthralling new world! Wonderful characters that charmed me from the beginning. Honestly this was a wonderfully perfect read to help me escape from the world for a bit.

Amazing (#3). I love this world and it's characters. Great storyline and well written. This series has been amazing to read. Definitely need to pick them up."

... Naomi ***** Amazon

"Yet again I'm absolutely totally blown away by this book (#4). I love the characters and the story line. Linda has written a fantastic book with steamy scenes that I didn't think were possible but brilliant. I loved the fact that we're now starting to see smaller named characters have a bigger role. It's very well written and can't wait to read more of the series."

*...Sam ***** Amazon*

Being an Indie Author

I've chosen to publish independently. This means I don't have the big machine of a traditional publishing company behind me. Reviews are very important on Amazon because they determine how visible you are in the marketplace. That makes your review, and every other review I receive, the most important tool in my marketing toolbox. If you've enjoyed reading this book, please consider spending a few minutes leaving me a review on Amazon. It doesn't have to be long.

Thank you!

See my website at www.lindaashtontrott.com to join the mailing list. You will not be inundated with mail, I promise! It will let you know when the latest book is released and if there are freebies.

Visit my Amazon author's page at https://www.amazon.com/~/e/B09TG29J19